# THE INTERSTELLAR SLAYER

## SPACE ASSASSINS 1

### SCOTT BARON

*"The two most powerful warriors are Patience and Time."*

*— Leo Tolstoy*

# CHAPTER ONE

The entirety of Emmik Rostall's compound was in a state of panic. The emmik was a powerful man, after all, and this simply should *not* happen. His magic might not have been as strong as a visla's, but he played an important role in the Council of Twenty's affairs, steering resources and coin with unrivaled skill.

As such, Emmik Rostall could afford a great deal of protection. Yet, despite all of the armed men and magical wards placed around his grounds and residence chambers, one of his men had been killed. And not by accident. This was the work of an assassin.

It was pure luck that led to the discovery of the body. On any other day no one would have been entering the small storage room where the slain guard's body had been stashed. His disappearance had gone unnoted, and not a sound had been heard, despite the proximity of so many others.

"A Wampeh Ghalian, Emmik. I would bet my life on it," the captain of the guard informed his employer.

"You're certain?" Rostall replied.

"The skill with which it was carried out leaves few alternatives."

"Then we seem to have quite a problem on our hands."

"Indeed, Emmik."

Emmik Rostall thought a long moment. For one of the legendary assassins to slay a member of his guard could only mean one thing. Someone had employed them to eliminate him. But, thanks to a bit of luck, the plot had been discovered before they could complete their task.

The smug power user smiled. He had an idea. "Call all of the inner estate guards to the center courtyard. Those already patrolling the perimeter will double their detail and not only keep an eye not only for intruders, but also upon on another."

"I will make it so," the captain replied, then rushed off to set the plan in motion.

Wampeh were a pale race with dark hair, easy to spot in a crowd in most instances. But Wampeh *Ghalian* were something else altogether. A rare anomaly of magical potential that allowed a fraction of a fraction of their kind to steal another's magic. Not by spells, but by drinking their blood.

It was a horrifying enough trait on its own. But the thousands of years they had worked as assassins, refining their craft until they became the single most feared group of hired killers the galaxy had ever seen, had granted them special talents. Expert use of shimmer cloaks, hiding themselves from view with the magical camouflage rendering them invisible, for one. Stealth unlike any other. And the most terrifying, the perfection of magical disguise spells far superior to any other.

That meant the killer could conceivably be anyone in the grounds. A powerful visla would be able to see through the disguise, but he was less powered, a mere emmik. At least Emmik Rostall knew the assassin was not his captain. For if it had been, despite his relatively impressive power, he would almost certainly already be dead.

The men patrolling the grounds were unlikely to be a disguised assassin. If someone had already been slain deep within the compound walls, it meant the threat was much closer than that. Still, having the guards checking one another provided an additional layer of scrutiny that might catch the Wampeh if he or she were to slip up.

A short while later, inside the deepest, most secure part of the compound, the emmik's guards stood at attention, row upon row of dangerous men of a number of races, armed with both blades and konuses, the magically charged bands snug around their wrists. The emmik had spared little expense in assembling those who would protect him within his walls, and all were well versed in the use of their magical weapons as well as conventional ones.

"The men are assembled, Emmik," the captain said, taking his place at his employer's side.

Emmik Rostall stepped up onto the slightly raised podium upon which his seat resided and surveyed the men before him. He then opened a little box beside his chair and removed a small, ornate vial. It was no longer than perhaps the tip of his fingers to his palm and the diameter of a woman's thumb. The top possessed a magically sealed nozzle, firmly in place for many, many years.

"Well, well. The time has finally come," he quietly murmured, studying the priceless relic in his hands.

Then Emmik Rostall quietly spoke the words that released the spell and popped the nozzle open with his finger. He slowly walked toward the first row of men standing quietly at attention.

Casually, and without warning, he splashed a drop of the tube's contents on the face of the first man he came to. The guard stood stock-still, the rivulet of water slowly running down his cheek. Rostall nodded then continued down the ranks, pausing every so often to flick his wrist again, sending a drop of water flying onto another of his men.

Not everyone received that treatment, though. The container didn't hold nearly enough of the priceless, irreplaceable fluid for all of the guards. And even if it did, Emmik Rostall's unpredictable use of the water was enough, he hoped, to perhaps make the hidden threat slip up.

The emmik wove through the ranks, following no set pattern, his captain close at his side, senses on high alert, killing spells ready to fly at a moment's notice. The stakes were higher than they'd ever been, and this was where he would earn his keep or die in the process.

The power user stopped abruptly in front of a man whose face seemed familiar, yet not. He was middle-aged and square-jawed. A medium shade of green to his skin. A Tslavar mercenary in his ranks. Quite a few of the combative race were among his men, their willingness to fight for coin making them a useful tool for far more than simple guard duties.

The man continued to look straight ahead, as did the others around him. Rostall stared hard, employing a little magical trick to make the object of his scrutiny a bit more uncomfortable than usual. The artery in the man's neck, however, did not beat any faster than normal.

Without warning, the emmik spun and splashed the guard to the man's right. The water had barely contacted his cheek when he let out a piercing cry and burst into flames. The other men jumped back, despite their training, shocked at what had just occurred.

In an instant the guard's screams evaporated into the plume of smoke that rose from the pile of smoldering ashes where he had been standing.

"I knew it! A Wampeh Ghalian in our midst!" The emmik cackled with glee. "And I killed him! Let it be known far and wide, even the Wampeh Ghalian are no match for the great Emmik Rostall."

He capped the vial and shook it, listening to the faint slosh of its contents. He had used nearly all of the waters, and their acquisition had cost more than the value of some lesser planets.

But the expenditure had been worth it. A fail-safe for just this sort of occasion. Only Wampeh Ghalian were affected by the waters, and as all had just seen, that reaction was as swift as it was violent.

Emmik Rostall tossed the vial in the air with exaggerated nonchalance, then caught it and slid the remaining Balamar waters into his pocket as if it were no big deal. He was playing it up for his men, knowing full well the Council of Twenty had eyes everywhere.

"Well done, sir," the captain said. "Shall I summon the outer guards next?"

"No need, Captain. Wampeh Ghalian always work alone. I have eliminated the would-be killer. Send the men back to their posts," he said, strolling to leave the chamber with the air of a man who hadn't a care in the world.

Oh, yes. Word of his prowess under duress, and against a Wampeh Ghalian, no less, would spread. In short order, the talk would reach the upper ranks of the Council of Twenty. He couldn't brag. That would be too obvious. But a seemingly organic boost to his standing would be a welcome thing.

"Oh, and please return this to its container and place it back in my chambers," he said, turning and tossing the vial to the captain.

The man, despite his years of military and martial experience, was nevertheless unnerved having an item that was worth more than he and everyone he ever knew would earn in their lifetimes so casually thrown to him.

"Of course, Emmik," he replied without so much as a flinch.

The emmik's actions would be reported, no doubt, but so might his. With Council eyes, one never could tell, and for that reason, it was important to always be on one's best behavior.

Rostall, for his part, felt an aching tug when the vial left his hand, but to complete the illusion, he had to make it seem like no big thing.

"I shall be in my study. Inform the chef I will dine in an hour."

"It will be done as you request," the captain said. He turned to the men, once again assembled and rigid, a gap in their lines where the immolated assassin's remains smoked on the ground. "The rest of you, get back to your duties."

The men scattered, relieved to be free of the emmik's precarious situation. Most returned to their tasks, others made for their quarters, their duty shifts having ended during the ordeal. The threat had passed, and they were safe. The emmik had seen to that.

One guard, however, casually made his way to a quiet area away from the others. The place he had stashed the other body. The one whose identity he had stolen.

The emmik was right. Wampeh Ghalian worked alone almost exclusively. However, this occasion was different. The young Wampeh had worked hard for many, many years to reach this point, and it had finally been time for his last test, observed by one of the five masters who had overseen the final years of his training. It was to be a trial by fire. And he had failed.

*Balamar waters?* he mused. *Who would have thought a mere emmik would possess them?*

Master Hozark sighed. All of those years of training were for naught. Gone in an instant. But he would not mourn the youth. It was not the Ghalian way. He would, however, honor his sacrifice in a different way.

He would complete the mission.

# CHAPTER TWO

The target of this particular assassination was a truly reprehensible man. While he seemed to be merely an emmik of some moderate power and status to most, he was truly a dynamo of damaging energy, his skills furthering the Council of Twenty's ever-expanding conquest of inhabited systems.

His magic was decently strong, but he was nowhere near as powerful as the many vislas who oversaw the Council's main affairs. *Their* powers were substantial. Those men and women were simply of a different class. But Emmik Rostall knew his place and had thrived in it.

Over the years, he had proven himself a valuable asset indeed, and while he didn't sit on the Council itself, he was well known to all twenty of its leaders, and his services were often relied upon. His loss would cause a ripple within the Council's affairs, the expanding impact hindering many of their plans already in motion.

It was for these reasons the Wampeh Ghalian had accepted the contract. Despite being assassins, they were not indiscriminate killers. There were plenty of mercenaries who would take any job for enough coin, but the Ghalian were different. Hard to contact and even harder to employ. It was why they'd survived as an order over millennia, and no one knew exactly what determined whether they did or did not accept a job. Only the Wampeh Ghalian themselves could answer that question.

The truth of the matter was, the pale assassins had long had their fingers in countless conflicts, steering them as their leadership saw fit while never taking sides. At least, not overtly. The Wampeh Ghalian never went to war, nor did they declare allegiances to any particular side. They simply accepted or declined a request as they saw fit.

The cost of their services was high. Higher than most could pay. But once engaged, they rarely failed. And in this instance, though the aspiring assassin tasked with the killing had fallen to the Balamar waters' deadly effect, the man who had helped train him would finish his assignment.

That the contract they'd accepted happened to fall within the Ghalian's sphere of interest had been fortuitous, and the elimination of Emmik Rostall, while difficult, would disrupt the Council's plans in dozens of systems. And that was reason enough, though they'd never admit as much.

The Balamar waters would be an issue, though.

Master Hozark was still amazed that the emmik had even managed to come by such a rare item. More so that he had deployed it in such a clever manner. Of course, a Wampeh Ghalian would remain calm in the face of death, but the man's attempts to spook his would-be assassin were quite ingenious. Master Hozark, however, was not one to spook. Not easily. Not ever, in fact. Not even when his associate had immolated and been reduced to a pile of ashes beside him.

Those damned waters hadn't been intended for such a use, but intentions do not always match results.

The man who had created them was no more than a long-deceased legend. A visla of extraordinary powers who had discovered a way to channel the life-giving and power-enhancing qualities of a rare healing water on his homeworld into something far more. Concentrated over the years, refined and increased in potency, the Balamar waters had granted those who came in contact with them not only health and longevity—the waters able to heal most wounds—they had also become a favorite restorative of a rather rare group of beings.

Zomoki.

Dragons, people in a distant galaxy would call them. Space dragons, to be exact. And while the Zomoki could travel through space, using their innate magical powers to jump from system to system, only a fraction of a percent of them were born with the true gift. That of intellect.

The Old Ones, also called the Wise Ones, were a small group of Zomoki who could not only utilize their kind's powerful magic, but also communicate with those they chose to. An evolved being with a sharp mind, unlike their base brethren who lived only to kill and burn and eat.

But that friendship with Visla Balamar, and their access to his waters, had ended badly when the last of the Old Ones who had bonded with the visla were killed along with him in the final days of the Council of Twenty's greatest conflict thus far.

They had been unable to recruit the visla to their ranks, and that could not be allowed to stand. So, rather than leave him to his own devices, the Council attempted to overthrow him and take his waters by force. With the aid of his Zomoki friends, however, the powerful visla had fought them off, and with relative ease.

It was then that the Council had made a decision. One that would have lasting repercussions.

It had cost much. Nearly all of the powerful Ootaki hair they possessed, in fact. The magic-bearing locks of the enslaved race that the Council possessed were almost entirely used up in the mass casting of one of the most destructive spells ever seen in the galaxy.

It was scorched earth tactics, both figuratively and literally, yet the visla and the Old Ones had very nearly withstood it. But the combined power of the strongest members of the Council had been multiplied with the addition of the Ootaki hair power, and when Balamar's defenses fell, it had been catastrophic.

A fifty-mile circle of destruction reduced what had been a thriving realm full of power and beauty on his world to a barren, red-sand wasteland. Only shattered fragments of the once-great estate remained.

The Council had accomplished their aim, killing the visla with an utterly enormous display of power. But they had lost their prize in the process. The Balamar waters they so very much wished to claim for their own were destroyed, the cistern in which they slowly accumulated and condensed their magical power lost forever.

Only a few possessed portions of those waters, and they became priceless in an instant.

And while they could heal those whom they touched, to drink them was certain death for all. And when it came to the Wampeh Ghalian, the waters were the one thing that could kill them on contact, the healing powers being quite the opposite to their pale flesh.

Like a vampire with holy water, the Wampeh Ghalian had avoided the Balamar waters quite successfully in the past. But with them long gone, Hozark had not anticipated a surprise reappearance, especially at such an inopportune time. But things happened, and not always the way he would have wished.

The pale man with high cheekbones and dark hair shed his disguise, letting the visage of the dead Tslavar guard he'd taken fall away. He was a master of the order, and shedding one magical deception for another was as natural to him as breathing. But more than just appearances, it was the behavior of a man that truly fooled people. That made a disguise complete.

It was something you had to inhabit fully, down to the very look in your eyes. It had to be *perfect*. Especially in his line of work.

Hozark slid his konus onto his wrist. The metal band looked as unassuming as most run-of-the-mill models did. But unlike the typical konus used by the emmik's men, this was a far more potent magic storage device. In fact, fully charged, Hozark's was capable of powering dozens of high-caliber spells.

Today, however, it held just enough magic to help the assassin complete his task. No more than that. Hozark was not worried, though. He was a man of great skill, and even fully absent of magic and minimally armed, he could eliminate a roomful of guards if it came down to it. But the konus would be welcome help.

A Wampeh Ghalian would absorb and utilize the power of those they fed on, but the emmik surrounded himself with unpowered men. While Hozark retained a bit of magic from his last job, he had been forced to rid himself of any excess that might draw the emmik's attention. He couldn't be sure the man even possessed such capabilities, but it was better safe than sorry in his line of work.

Security was tight in the estate, and with the numerous magical wards the emmik had placed at random locations, Hozark and his young associate were unable to bring so much as an enchanted blade without risk of premature discovery. Only a basic konus would be able to pass without raising an alarm, and that was an oversight on the emmik's part. He simply never expected one to be used against him in his own home.

Hozark strode quickly through the grounds, maintaining his new disguise as he prepared for a most dangerous detour from his original plan. There was Balamar water present, and he would have to address that problem before he could move forward. Anything less was suicide, and while he had made plenty of deaths seem to be just that, he had no desire of meeting his own fate.

# CHAPTER THREE

The captain of the guard was still in possession of the Balamar waters when the disguised assassin came upon him sitting on a low seat outside of Rostall's chambers. His master had told him to return the strange container to them. He simply hadn't said when, exactly.

The captain was turning the vial over in his hands, studying it with great curiosity. He had removed it from its box, but Hozark could see the little spout was still sealed and the man's skin was dry. He hadn't touched it. Good. An enemy in possession of the Balamar waters was dangerous enough, but one with the powerful liquid on his hands could land a killing blow without even meaning to.

"Why aren't you at your station, Beitsal?" the captain asked the disguised man, rising to his feet as he approached.

"I was sent to find you, Captain," the assassin replied, moving closer. "There's a pressing matter that needs your attention."

He was almost upon the man when a flicker of doubt flashed across the captain's face. He scrutinized the man before him, but the disguise was perfect. But the man sensed *something*, and

Hozark saw the attack in his eyes before he even moved. This one was still on alert, regardless of his emmik's confidence.

The captain lashed out with a dagger, deftly whipped from its sheath even as he thumbed open the vial in his hand and moved to splash the would-be killer.

Hozark lunged in fast, his forearm blocking the captain's motion, sending the deadly spray of water just wide of the assassin's cheek. It was so close he could feel the charged waters move the air beside him. He'd been inches from death before, but never from this particular weapon.

The captain was quick, though, and with all of Hozark's efforts aimed at avoiding the instant death of the waters, a far slower variety lunged forward. The captain was a man of exceptional skill, Hozark admired, even as he felt the blade plunge into his abdomen.

This was not good.

If this had been an attempt against an underpowered and non-Council-connected target, he would have had healing salves and magical dressings with him. He bore many scars from their previous use over his lengthy career. But he had been unable to bring such magical accoutrements with him to the emmik's estate.

With a quickness that seemed almost unnatural to the captain of the guard, Hozark drove his own unenchanted blade deep into the man's torso, ending the fight in an instant. The captain fell to the ground, the vial of deadly waters dropping from his unclenched hand. The assassin had avoided certain death by it, but the damage had been done. The wound the blade had opened was deep, and it would definitely be a problem.

Hozark staunched the bleeding as best he could with a makeshift dressing and a binding spell, but the injury was a nasty one. He was going to have to work fast.

Shifting his plans, thanks to this unwelcome bit of bad luck, he cut a thick swatch of cloth from the dead man's garb and carefully picked up the vial, tucking it in the dead man's pocket. He then wasted some of the precious power in his konus to levitate the dead captain into a nearby storage chamber. He then stashed his body in what appeared to be an under-utilized section of the room.

He hoped his assessment was correct. The corpse would be found far too soon for his liking, but by the time that happened, he'd either have completed the task, or be dead. There was nothing else to do but press on.

The master assassin shed his disguise and donned a new one, assuming the appearance of the captain of the guard. He'd observed the man long enough to have a good handle on his mannerisms. Hopefully good enough for what needed to be done. It would not be an easy kill now that he had no time to prepare. He would have to improvise.

There wasn't much in the room that would be of use to him. Nothing to craft into another weapon, just some furnishings, linen, and an assortment of disused storage vessels. One of them caught his eye. A small bottle, likely having contained a potion at one time or another.

"Hmm. It might just work," the assassin mused as a novel idea hit him.

With great care, he once again plucked the vial of Balamar waters from the dead man's possession, drawing it from his pocket and carrying it to the little basin in the room, picking up the small empty bottle on the way. A jug of water rested on a nearby table, a layer of dust floating on its surface. It seemed his initial impression of the disused nature of the room appeared to be correct.

Ever so carefully, he opened the top of the vial and emptied its contents into the bottle, then closed its lid, sealing it with a trio of spells to ensure it would not open accidentally. He then slid the liquid death into his pocket and proceeded to cast a simple fire spell.

No smoke was produced by the magical flame, but the heat was sufficient to cause the residual Balamar waters to evaporate, eventually. It took far longer than it would have with regular water, though, the magical powers of the waters making it particularly difficult to destroy them. But, eventually, a fine wisp of steam rose from the vial as the last traces of the waters evaporated into nothingness.

Hozark had been very careful not to damage the vial in the process, maintaining a temperature just low enough to keep it intact. He reached out with his senses, passing his hand close to the still-warm vessel. As a Wampeh Ghalian, he would feel the waters if any trace remained. There was not a single hit on his internal radar.

Satisfied that he had succeeded, Hozark picked up the vial with his bare hand. If he had been mistaken, at least his death would come quickly, if not painlessly.

Nothing happened.

"Excellent," he quietly said, then picked up the water vessel on the nearby table and poured a small amount into the now-sterile vial.

He closed the top and splashed a drop on his hand. The nozzle hadn't warped from the heat, he was pleased to note. Master Hozark moved a little too quickly and winced. The injury seemed to be even worse than he had thought. He quickly reapplied the binding spell to his wound and stepped out into the corridor. There was no time to waste.

He hurried toward where he felt reasonably certain the master of the estate would be. He had many private rooms in which to reside, but after his recent brush with an assassin, and given his ego, he felt the man would wish to remain visible to his staff for a while to show he was unafraid. Rounding the corner, he saw he was correct.

The emmik was in his open receiving chamber, six of his finest guards spread around the room. All had been present when Hozark's young associate had been killed. In his wounded state, there was no way he could get to the emmik before the guards were upon him. And slowed as he was, there was a very real chance their interference would give the emmik the time he needed to react.

He could attempt to kill the man outright, of course. But it was likely to end with his demise as well, and to carry out the task and survive was his principal goal. Suicide was not something a Wampeh Ghalian had any interest in, unless it was the appearance of one they were planting on their victim's corpse.

"Emmik, there is another assassin on the grounds!" the disguised Wampeh shouted out as he rushed into the room.

The guards knew their duties well, each falling in close to the emmik, surrounding him, weapons drawn and ready, but spaced out just far enough as to prevent a single attacker from taking them down. The captain had trained his men well, he grudgingly admired.

No, he definitely couldn't take them all fast enough. So Hozark made straight for them instead, pulling the ornate vial from his pocket with a flourish so they could clearly see it in his hand. He thumbed open the stopper and quickly splashed a drop on each of the men, some of the water getting on his own hand in the process.

The emmik saw this and nodded approvingly. He hated to lose any more of the precious fluid, but if there was truly a second assassin, he was in even more jeopardy than he had realized.

"Sir, we must get you to safety until we know how many there are!" Hozark said.

Reluctantly, the emmik agreed. He hated to have an underling do his dirty work for him, but the captain had served him well for some time. Also, his own survival was more important than appearances at the moment.

"Of course. To my private quarters," the man commanded.

The guards took off at a quick pace, creating a flesh-and-blood shield around their employer.

"You two. Inside with the emmik. You four, stand guard outside the door. Be on high alert. These Wampeh Ghalian are tricky bastards," the assassin said, then closed the door behind him.

In the much smaller room, the two guards in the room had done what Hozark had hoped they would. They had taken positions very close to the emmik. Too close. Emmik Rostall looked at his captain with satisfaction at his underling's performance. He had done well and would need to receive some sort of accolade for his quick work and attention to the matter.

Then he noticed the blood faintly seeping through his shirt.

Hozark caught the glance and flash of surprise on the man's face, but he was already in motion long before it, his blades flashing out and dropping both guards with ease, now that they stood so close together. An instant later, his fangs had sunk deep into the emmik's neck, choking off the killing spell rising to his lips.

No matter a man's power, the words had to be spoken in order to cast. And the crushing strength of the Wampeh's jaws combined with the sudden blood loss were enough to choke off the spell before its completion.

Hozark felt Rostall's power flow into his body with every greedily taken drop of blood. *This* was the true power of a Wampeh Ghalian. This rarest of traits that only a fraction of a percent of an even smaller fraction of a percent of Wampeh possessed. And even then, of those, only a handful had the drive and force of will to become a Ghalian assassin.

The man's life force flickered, then extinguished. Hozark pulled his lips from the dead man's neck. There was no taking power from a dead man, and Wampeh Ghalian never drank from any but power users. To do so was not only pointless, it was also distasteful. Only those with power ever met this sort of fate.

But the Ghalian didn't let the public know that. The frightful legends of the deadly assassins who sucked you dry went far in bolstering their reputations.

Hozark focused his newly stolen powers inward, reciting his most powerful healing spells. With an irritating, itchy tingle, the wound sealed, the damage knitting itself into a small line of knotted flesh. He could have continued, leaving little to no trace on his body, but he didn't want to waste any more of the stolen power than necessary.

It would be just another scar to add to the collection, and as he didn't know how much more of the stolen power he would need to use to make his escape, prudence was the only option. For now, the guards stationed just outside were his concern. He would worry about the rest after he'd taken care of them.

The disguised assassin wiped the blood from his lips, hid the bodies as best he could, then walked to the door, finally feeling like himself again, his body healed, and a potent, stolen power flowing through him.

"You four, come here. The emmik requires your presence," the apparent captain of the guard said, stepping aside to let the men enter.

It was a room they would not exit alive.

# CHAPTER FOUR

Hozark only had to dispose of a half dozen men as he made his escape from the innermost chambers of the power user's home. He'd have much preferred avoiding any further bloodshed at all, but sneaking out unnoticed was simply not an option. Not with the guards on high alert after the attempt on their master's life.

Little did they know, Emmik Rostall's body was already growing cold in his private quarters, along with those of his closest personal guards.

He had mowed the men down quickly as he rushed from the grounds as fast as he was able without raising more attention. He wished he had been able to bring a shimmer cloak with him on this mission. Being able to render himself invisible to all but the most adept power users would have been a useful tool to have right about now.

But there was no sense lamenting what simply could not be. He would have to make do. And that meant bloodshed.

Fortunately, with Emmik Rostall's power now coursing through his body, rendering him whole once more, Hozark was at least able to make quick work of those he did have to eliminate. No unnecessary delays with that lot. Just fast and ruthless slaying of those obstructing his escape, followed by only the most perfunctory hiding of the bodies. They would be found soon, no doubt. But Hozark would be long gone by then.

Getting clear of the estate's buildings, finally safe out in the sprawling grounds, Hozark at last allowed himself to take a breath. It had been a high-tension situation for much longer than he would have preferred, and despite his training, expertise, and stolen power, it was exhausting nevertheless. The sooner he could be clear of the whole damned system, the better.

Fortunately, he had just the ticket for that.

While a shimmer cloak was impractical for the work he and his young aspiring assassin had been doing within the power user's walls, outside was another matter entirely. The magic was very costly, and it required the talents of a highly skilled caster. It just so happened, all Wampeh Ghalian were drilled in those arcane and difficult spells from the earliest days of their training, making them second nature by the time they rolled out on actual assassinations.

Using a shimmer cloak on a person was one thing. Making one work to hide an entire ship, even one of the Wampeh Ghalian's small insertion craft, was no easy task, and the magic was quite uncommon. Some mercenaries utilized it, as did magic users with enough power to spare. But for most, it was simply impossible, and a poorly cast shimmer was almost worse than none at all.

Hozark was nearly through the copse of woods that separated him from his hidden craft when the alarm rang out from the estate.

"Damn. That was sooner than expected," he grumbled, increasing his pace.

It seemed someone had stumbled upon one of his victims—perhaps the emmik himself—and sounded the alarm. He would have to hurry.

Weaving through the trees, the deadly assassin raced toward the seemingly empty clearing where his ship resided, cloaked and waiting for him. He checked the layers of magical wards he and his deceased friend had laid around it. None had been disturbed. The ship was safe and undiscovered.

Without further ado, he incanted the spell required to drop the shimmer cloaking long enough to find and step into the craft's waiting door. He knew where the ship was even with the spell engaged, of course, as any Ghalian master would. But given the injury he'd sustained, he was not going to slow his egress any more than absolutely necessary. He deemed the extra seconds he would lose making sure he didn't run face-first into the door unacceptable.

Hozark sealed the ship's door behind him, then reactivated the shimmer spell. A second later, the ship once again blended into the area around it. Next, the Wampeh hurried to the command seat and released the personalized spell that protected his Drookonus. Without it, his ship would never fly.

The Drooks were akin to the Ootaki as a race. Unlike the golden-haired men and women who were prized for the magic-storing capabilities of their hair––a huge amount of power they were unable to use themselves––these were specialized magic casters of very specific, yet quite considerable power. They could make things fly.

Nearly all Drooks were enslaved from birth into a life of servitude powering all manner of craft. Their flight magic was as strong as it was unique, and it was the basis of space travel across all the known systems in the galaxy, with the exception of Zomoki. The dragon creatures had their own magic that allowed the more powerful of them to jump from world to world.

But Zomoki power was untappable, and maintaining a stable of Drooks while on often long and dangerous assassination contracts was simply untenable. Thus,

Drookonuses were used. It was quite an expensive item, and utterly necessary.

The simple-looking rod cost more than most would see in a lifetime, and it possessed the power of a great many Drooks stored within. This allowed for craft to be powered without active Drooks aboard.

Few possessed the skill to make a truly powerful Drookonus, adding to their value and rarity. But the Wampeh Ghalian were a very, very old and very, very wealthy order. Though not extravagant people by any means, for things they deemed necessary to complete their goals, coin was not an issue.

Hozark powered up the craft and immediately took off skyward. He popped up beyond the canopy of trees around him just in time to see the swarming ships spewing out from the emmik's estate. With the speed and frantic nature of their launch, the assassin mused that they must have found their leader's body already. Once more, bad luck was following him on this contract.

There were a lot of ships in the air already, and more were launching. Far more than he'd have expected of any normal emmik. But Rostall appeared to have been of even greater use to the Council of Twenty than the assassin had originally believed, given the sheer quantity of resources at his disposal.

Even with a shimmer cloak engaged, he would have to fly very carefully. With that many opposing vessels in the sky, one misstep could spell disaster.

"It has certainly been an experience, my friends," he said as he maneuvered around the moving slalom course of enemy craft, like an airborne skier racing through a multi-planed series of gates.

For in flight, nothing was a simple straight line. All directions were in play. A talented pilot, as well as master killer, Hozark was unconcerned. This part was easy compared to the rest.

He stayed low, noting the upward path of the majority of the blockading ships. Apparently, they were trying to keep any from flying toward the safety of the darkness above. It was a sound plan, for a normal adversary, that is. But Hozark was not such an opponent, and he skimmed the treetops as he flew past the edges of the emmik's domain, putting a great deal of distance between himself and its borders before blasting up toward space.

Once safely in the inky vacuum, he engaged his ship's magical jump and was gone.

# CHAPTER FIVE

Hozark's craft emerged from its jump in a crowded system, his shimmer cloak dropped well before arrival. For any who observed his ship, there was nothing out of the ordinary to see.

He could have kept the shimmer engaged during and after the jump, but to do so would not only use a huge amount of magic, it would also make his pending rendezvous a bit more difficult. When de-cloaking a vessel, you had to be absolutely certain you were not noted by any curious eyes, and this system was chosen specifically for how busy it was.

He blended in just fine.

"Uzabud, are you present?" he signaled over his skree.

"Hey, Hozark. Glad to hear you made it back in one piece," a gruff voice answered a moment later over their magical comms device. "I'm standing by in orbit behind the little moon above Sokhar, as agreed. You coming straight here, or do you have other business in the system first?"

"Stay there. I will join you momentarily," Hozark replied, cutting off his skree call and directing his ship toward Uzabud's location.

Uzabud had been a space pirate for a number of years before

venturing out to make his own way. That way was one full of smuggling, thievery, and all manner of nefarious dealings. It was after many years establishing something of a name for himself in that arena that he and Hozark had first crossed paths. He'd been an ally ever since.

The chatterbox pirate was a handful at times, and his incessant banter could be exhausting. But he *always* came through. And over the years, he and Hozark had cemented a lasting friendship. In fact, outside of his Ghalian brothers and sisters, Bud was the most trusted of Hozark's associates.

And it was Uzabud's unique skill set that would be employed today. Following an endeavor with as many potential pitfalls as Emmik Rostall's assassination would possess found Hozark requiring a new ship before returning to the Wampeh Ghalian training ground he was currently calling home base. And Bud was just the man to help.

It was likely overkill—a pun the order of assassins never laughed at—but *if* someone had seen his ship, no matter how unlikely, it would be a dangerous loose end that could prove problematic. He would retrieve his other ship from Bud, allowing the former pirate to stash his current ride away in one of his many secret hiding places until Hozark next required that particular craft.

Perhaps Hozark was being paranoid, but a healthy dose of paranoia often led to a longer life, especially in his line of work.

He took the roundabout way to their rendezvous point, making a lazy show of it, appearing to any who might be watching as if he was in no rush at all. The truth of the matter, however, was after that mess of a job, he just wanted to switch ships and be on his way as soon as possible. But, nevertheless, his lackadaisical approach looked anything but hurried.

"I am approaching on your left," Hozark informed his waiting friend as he leveled his little shimmer ship to match the orientation of the larger craft.

"I see you," Uzabud replied. "Glad you brought it back without any damage. *This* time."

"*That* was an unfortunate turn of events entirely beyond my control, as you well know, Bud."

"Yeah, I know. Just pulling your chain. Still, glad to see I won't be stuck fixing that thing up again."

"As am I, I assure you."

Bud laughed. "I'd assume so. Okay, swing around to your usual spot, and I'll see you in a minute."

The assassin approached the larger craft as he had done countless times before, docking with a soft magical seal among a small assortment of other lesser ships mounted on the vessel's hull. Say what you would about Uzabud's unusual ways, he was always prepared, and despite his jovial nature, his paranoia nearly rivaled that of his Wampeh friend.

Once the craft was secured, Hozark did a thorough once-over to ensure he had not left a single incriminating piece of evidence behind, just in case Uzabud ran into any trouble once they parted ways.

He then shouldered the small bag containing the items stolen and used in his hurried flight from Emmik Rostall's estate, pocketed his Drookonus rod, and stepped into Bud's ship, sealing his doorway behind him. The walk to the common area was a short one, and the ship's captain was waiting for him. Along with a new, unfamiliar face.

"There he is!" Bud said with a big grin.

If not for the fact that his friend was one of the deadliest men in twenty systems, he'd perhaps have even considered giving him a hug. But, that wasn't Hozark's style, even with his closest associates.

"Where's Enok?" the former pirate asked.

"Not coming," he replied.

An uncomfortable silence hung in the air a moment. It wasn't the first time someone had been lost on a mission. It sometimes happened in their line of work. But Bud knew this was different. This was a Wampeh Ghalian they were talking about, and one Hozark had spent considerable time training.

The pirate's eyes drifted down to the bloodstains on Hozark's tunic.

"Yours?" he asked, shifting the subject.

"It was a rushed job," the Wampeh replied, not exactly answering, but appearing to be in perfect health.

"Care to tell me about it?"

"Not particularly."

Bud nodded pensively. "Anyone important?"

"All lives are important, my friend," the assassin replied.

"I couldn't agree more," the newcomer interjected.

He was a relatively young man. Perhaps thirty years, give or take. But his eyes possessed a confidence of one far older. Hozark reached out with his Wampeh Ghalian senses, probing him for signs of danger. None were to be found.

"Sorry, I forgot to introduce you two," Uzabud said. "Hozark, this is Laskar, my new copilot."

"You don't fly with a copilot, Bud."

"Well, not usually. But when I scored this one, I couldn't pass on the opportunity. He's one hell of a pilot—"

"You're damn right, I am," the rather cocky man interjected.

"Though a bit of a prick at times," Uzabud added.

"Hey!"

"And, get this. He even possesses a little magic of his own."

That tidbit caught Hozark's attention. He hadn't sensed anything from the man. "Oh?" he said, curiously, reaching out and probing once again as he focused his attention more fully on the man. Yes. There it was. Just a faint shimmer of power.

"It's just a tiny amount of magic," Laskar said. "Even a child's konus could do more, I'd wager."

"Go on, show him something," Bud urged.

"Well, okay," he said, then cast a rather basic levitation spell, moving a storage bin across the compartment. He had done so without using a konus to power the spell, so he definitely possessed power. But Hozark was most certainly not impressed.

"Ah, yes. That was very well done," the Wampeh said as politely as he could.

Sure, there was some power there, but it appeared to be so little an amount he wouldn't even bother draining the man if he had been a target. Still, if Uzabud vouched for him, he must be a competent pilot. Better than that, even. Maybe even living up to his cockiness. For the ship's captain notoriously worked alone, as did his Wampeh friend.

Hozark handed over the bag from his shoulder. "Here. Perhaps you can fetch some coin for these."

Uzabud glanced inside. Weapons, mostly. Items taken during the completion of the contract, no doubt.

"You could at least have cleaned the blood off of them," he griped.

"You do not want them?"

"I didn't say that," Bud shot back.

Hozark snorted with amusement. The stolen blades and other improvised weapons would clean up easily, and Bud would make a nice profit from them. It was a bonus he was glad to pay the man, and far better it come from Emmik Rostall's coffers than his own coin.

"The ship's ready whenever you want it," Bud said. "You wanna maybe go down to Sokhar and have some drinks before you head out?"

"Not this time, I'm afraid," Hozark said.

Uzabud wasn't surprised one bit. A Wampeh Ghalian had just been lost, and Hozark would be anxious to return to the other masters to report in. But he had to ask. The semblance of normalcy in a difficult time.

Hozark turned and strode off to the new ship awaiting him. "Until next time, my friend," he called back over his shoulder.

"Don't be a stranger," Bud called in reply.

"Nice meeting you," Laskar added.

Hozark went straight to his craft, took his Drookonus from his pocket, and quickly powered up the vessel, setting the spells for flight in motion. He then buzzed around to the other side of the small moon. But he didn't jump away. Not just yet. First, he had something he needed to do.

The assassin cast a dozen variants of spells, checking the craft for any signs of trackers, wards, or unwanted magic that may have been hidden aboard, just in case. The new copilot seemed all right, but until he had fully vetted the man himself, prudence was called for.

"Clean," he noted with satisfaction after the final spell.

Hozark then slid into the contoured pilot's seat and pulled from the Drookonus's power. A moment later, the ship jumped away, vanishing in a flash.

# CHAPTER SIX

Hozark did not delay in his return to the training facility on the small world of Sarlik. While he might have normally made a stop or two along the way following a particularly difficult contract, this was something different. He had lost his pupil, and the training house needed to know.

The Wampeh Ghalian had many such locales hidden across the systems. Each appeared to be a normal building from the outside, but within there lay a deeply camouflaged house of the deadliest assassins in the known galaxy and their aspiring young trainees.

Aside from those residing inside, the layers upon layers of defensive spells cast into the fabric of the building every time a Ghalian entered or exited had created a protective shielding of so many layers that penetration would be near impossible for even the most powerful of vislas.

The Sarlik location had been Hozark's main base of operations for several years, though he visited others often, and a good many young Wampeh had risen to the ranks of full-fledged Ghalian under his watchful tutelage. The five masters were never residing at any training house at the same time, but they did overlap in their visitations fairly often.

Such instances were a boon to the pupils, for they could watch firsthand how the best of the best could fight, their individual styles as varied as the men and women who made up that top tier. And that was a thing about the Wampeh Ghalian that made them so difficult to stop, even for the most highly trained warrior. The Ghalian might seem like they fought as most experienced in combative arts might, utilizing more than one style, as need dictated.

But beyond that, each of the assassins stretched their minds and skills in the final years of their progress toward full-fledged assassin. Not by practicing styles they'd committed to muscle memory in the years of grueling work, but by devising a new style entirely their own.

The masters helped them dial in their particular skills in the process, guiding them toward their ultimate goal. A fighting method that none outside of the order had encountered before. It was one of the things that made the Wampeh Ghalian nearly unstoppable.

The counterstrikes and counter-spells, drilled into soldiers so often they didn't even have to think to deploy them, were not effective against the assassins. In fact, knowing the pending defenses allowed the Ghalian to use those very counters against them.

But against Balamar waters? There was no defense or counter for a Wampeh Ghalian. Only death, as Enok had so recently learned.

"Hozark, I hear Emmik Rostall has fallen," Corann said by way of greeting as he entered the secret inner facility.

Hozark was one of the masters, but Corann was the head of The Five. The perfect, unexpected assassin. A middle-aged woman with a motherly smile who could kill a dozen men before they so much as considered reaching for a weapon.

"I see the network was waiting for us," Hozark said of the news that reached her before him.

Unlike traditional long-range skree communications, the Wampeh Ghalian almost exclusively utilized in-person relay of important information. Skree messages were secure and private, and there was absolutely no way they could be tapped into. Or so the general public believed.

The Wampeh Ghalian, however, were privy to a very well-kept secret. For a very, very select few in the Council of Twenty, there was a back door. One only a handful of people knew existed. One that allowed the eavesdropping of conversations, if the right spell were to be deployed. But one never knew when or where that might happen.

The master assassins, therefore, avoided them entirely for all but the most benign communications.

"Yes," Corann said. "Word reached us an hour before your arrival. "But I see Enok is not with you. Was he delayed? Or...?"

"Sadly, Enok has left this life," Hozark replied, his jaw flexing slightly as the frustration within him made a quickly quashed attempt to assert itself. "It was... *unexpected*."

"Death usually is," Corann replied.

Hozark said nothing, but instead simply placed the small bottle in his pocket on the counter. Corann picked it up and reached out with her senses. She didn't panic and drop it when she realized its contents. No Ghalian master would. But her eyes did widen slightly.

"Balamar waters? In this day and age, *that* truly is unexpected. They are utterly priceless. Who could have foreseen a mere emmik possessing one of the last traces of them?"

"Indeed," Hozark agreed. "But Enok stood firm. His resolve never wavered. He did not even flinch as the waters hit him."

"A credit to our order."

"Yes. And his end was quick."

Only a few had ever seen the hell those waters could unleash in person. They were so rare that only tales were all most would ever hear. But the order now possessed a tiny quantity. A deadly weapon to be locked away in their secret vaults, safe from ever being used against them again.

"It seems you encountered quite a resistance. But you did well, and Rostall fell, in the end."

"I made sure of it," Hozark replied. "And with his demise, the Council of Twenty now has one less asset on the table. Of course, Visla Tumertz and the others waiting in the wings will step in to seize much of Rostall's business. And though he works with the Council, he is not connected as Rostall was. This will destabilize their operations for a little while, at least."

Corann smiled that funny little grin she had perfected over the years. "It is funny you should say that, Hozark."

"Oh?"

"Yes. For word is, a new threat is rising."

"So soon? Impossible."

"It seems someone else was waiting for this sort of opportunity to leverage their powers to further their aspirations. There is a power shift within the Council. And if it proceeds unchecked, it could send dozens of systems into chaos."

"What are the Council up to this time?" Hozark asked, unaccustomed to being out of the loop.

"We do not know for certain," Corann replied. "But our services have been retained, and at a great fee, no less, to ensure that this consolidation of power does not happen."

This troubled the assassin. It was all moving too fast for his liking. Things of this nature often did, of course, but something about the speed at which this was unfolding was unsettling.

"Why is this news only now reaching our ears?" he asked.

"It came to our attention while you and Enok were away completing your contract. It had taken one of our most deeply embedded spies months to be able to safely bring the information and contract request."

"So, it is verified and legit?"

"It is."

"Hmm. We proceed as employed, then."

"We do. Impartial and efficient. Whatever mess is stirring, the Wampeh Ghalian do not wage war, nor do we take sides."

Hozark chuckled. "We do not. But we do tip the scales from time to time."

"When it aligns with our desires," Corann replied with a grin. "In any case, the price has been paid, and we are engaged."

"Excellent. Shall I assume Varsuvala will be handling this? I know how she has been eager for more of a challenge after her last several contracts."

"No, Hozark. This particular target is not for her."

"Oh?"

"No. This one is for you."

"So soon after another high-profile contract? Of course, I am happy to oblige, but we spread these out for a reason."

"Yes, normally. But this one is most definitely for you," she replied. "And you will need a vespus blade."

At this, Hozark actually felt a flash of concern. Vespus blades were legendary weapons of the Wampeh Ghalian. A blue metal imbued with crackling, magical properties, and only crafted by less than a handful of surviving master artisans, and at great cost. If you could even find one of them, that is.

"A vespus blade?"

"Yes. You must find Mester Orkut. He is the finest of those few still breathing who possess the ability to craft one."

"This is an unusual request, Corann. What's wrong? Why a vespus blade, of all things? We haven't seen one since––"

"Because your target is very powerful."

"I can handle powerful."

"And he resides on Arkanis. Your home world."

Hozark was surprised. It was a cold, hard place he was born and had lived in before his innate talent was discovered and the Wampeh Ghalian took him into their fold. But even so, cold was an inconvenience that any of the order could deal with as easily as he could.

"I haven't been back since childhood, Corann. You know that. There is more, isn't there?" he asked. "Any one of us could handle this contract."

An unusual look flashed in Corann's eyes. Sympathy. And not the false kind she put on display for unsuspecting targets. It was disconcerting to say the least.

"He is protected," she said. "His right-hand man. Or, woman, to be exact. Someone we know. Someone we believed dead."

Hozark felt her words land like a punch to the gut. A sinking feeling of dread began to grow inside him. "Who, Corann?" he asked, though he already knew the impossible answer.

She saw the look in his eye and was sure he already knew. "Yes, Hozark. It is Samara. She lives. And at the time of her supposed demise, she possessed one of the last known vespus blades."

"I know it well."

"As you would. We thought it lost upon her death. With this news, we can only assume it is still in her possession. For this reason, you will need one of your own if you are to face her."

If the pale man weren't already of an alabaster complexion, he would certainly have become so. Oh, yes. He knew Samara well. *Quite* well. They had trained together from a young age, rising in the ranks of the Wampeh Ghalian as they blossomed from youth into adulthood.

They had even been lovers for a brief time. More than brief, truth be told, though members of their order never bonded. It simply wasn't done. Not because of an explicit rule, but because in their line of work one could not afford to have those sorts of weaknesses and attachments.

But they had come as close as you could without crossing that line before she had left on what seemed a relatively run-of-the-mill contract. And then she was dead. Or so they had all believed.

"I'll leave immediately," Hozark said, picking up the deadly little bottle of Balamar waters and sliding it back into his pocket, hoping he would not need it.

The master assassin was going home.

# CHAPTER SEVEN

Arkanis.

That cold, shitty planet he'd left behind all those years ago.

Hozark couldn't believe he was actually going to be returning to the small world tucked away in a black sun's solar system. It was never bright there. The perfect place for his pale race to thrive. The only illumination of any strength was of the magically created variety. Outside of that, it was a dark world.

The light spectrum emitted by the sun was well into the range beyond ultraviolet, but that wasn't all it did. The burning orb also threw off a strange power that could affect the casting of spells in wildly unpredictable ways if its solar magic was not taken into account.

Not many could benefit from that particular trait of his home system, but being a native son of the realm, Hozark had to admit, he had a bit of an advantage. He knew, for instance, that the glowing ripples of light that danced across the sky could, if a casting was timed just right, make a spell orders of magnitude more powerful than intended.

Or it could make it fail altogether. It was something of a crapshoot. Fortunately, this was not a daily occurrence.

The phenomenon was the byproduct of the sun's invisible energy flaring out and interacting with Arkanis's own magnetic field. A flowing aurora of clashing power blossoming colors across the dark skies when you least expected them. And being perpetually dark, the glow was visible whenever it visited.

Interestingly, some would complain of light pollution on the dark world, but not from the magically powered illumination, but rather the dancing aurora in the sky that often made stargazing near impossible.

The fact that there was no night and no day—at least, not in terms of sunrise and sunset—meant that businesses on Arkanis functioned on a somewhat odd schedule. Many locales were staffed around the clock, never closing, even into the wee hours of the night.

Others, staffed and run only by their proprietors, would shut their doors for a time to allow them to rest before reopening. For the most part, though, the hours on a clock were little more than a nuisance.

When Hozark had left that world, he had been no more than a boy. To be fair, he hadn't *left*, precisely. *Taken* would more accurately describe his departure. Taken by a thin, quiet man with a dangerous air to him and flown away from the only place he'd ever known.

Home was cold, and it was dark, but it was home nevertheless. The place that would become his new home was neither of those things, but it was uncomfortable just the same, albeit in a different manner.

The training house the lean Wampeh Ghalian had taken him to—Fahbahl, he learned the man was called—was anything but a place of comfort and leisure. It wasn't the facility itself that was difficult. It was the grueling training his unaccustomed body was subjected to.

"Your mind is your greatest weapon. And it is yours alone to wield. Learn to control it, and you shall do well. Fail to do so and you will not survive," Fahbahl said as he ushered him into the building. "But between you and me, I think you have it in you. Do not prove me wrong."

These were the last words of kindness he would hear from the man. From then on, the impassive mask of the Ghalian master was firmly in place.

The harshness of those first days had left him wondering if he might be killed by these strange new housemates. There were young boys and girls ranging in age from youths all the way to young adults, each of them flashing him unwelcome stares as he was ushered into their bunkhouse.

Later, he would realize it was simply the gaze of those who had already endured what he was about to. They had gone through the discomforts of those early days and weeks and knew full well what he was about to be subjected to.

Initially, he would be forced to stand still for hours upon hours, a painful spell striking him down if he so much as budged. It seemed a strange thing to practice, this motionless boredom, but the Ghalian appeared to place great importance on it. And so, he stood. For hours he stood. All day long, in fact, until he was finally allowed to move.

But that movement was not one of relaxation. It was one of speed and urgency. After so long trying to make himself like a statue, he was abruptly forced to run a small obstacle course in the far reaches of the chamber. There was a much more complex variant he saw the older aspirants working through, but in his weak state, the smaller one was more than an adequate challenge.

His body ached, and his emotions were raw after that first day, and the cool gaze from all of the other students did not help soothe the pain any. All of them save one, that is.

Samara was her name. A young girl of the same age who had

been brought in just days before him. She hadn't become like the others. Not yet, anyway. And it was her kindness––albeit doled out with great care not to be observed by the others––that helped him survive those first few days.

As they grew, Hozark and Samara found themselves consistently topping their classmates, struggling and eventually succeeding alongside one another through all of the rigorous levels of Ghalian training. It took many, many years of grueling labor, and they were no longer children when it finally happened, but, eventually, the pair graduated to full-fledged Wampeh Ghalian.

They had been lovers, from time to time, for several years by that point.

The pair had been careful to keep their dalliance secret, though the masters were well aware of it, regardless. So long as it remained an indulgence of the flesh alone, however, it would not be an issue. But it could not become more.

Wampeh Ghalian did not bond, for obvious reasons. It was simply unheard of, and the pair had no intention of violating that unspoken rule. But they had come as close as any had to crossing that line, despite each of their protests to the contrary.

They went their separate ways eventually, as was the Ghalian life, but their paths crossed often, and intentionally, more often than not. They were each other's touchstone. A grounding place to call home in a hostile galaxy.

And then Samara had died, her body scattered to the winds in a mission gone terribly wrong.

Or so they had all believed.

# CHAPTER EIGHT

Young Hozark had only been in the Ghalian training house for a few months when Master Garrusch, an older, craggy-faced Wampeh who had seen more than his share of combat in his lifetime, had commanded him to strip and wait for further instructions. It was cold, though the chamber was inside a climate-controlled facility, the spells keeping the temperature precisely where the masters wished it to be.

And today, they wished it to be cold. Fortunately, he had been raised on Arkanis and was used to protecting himself from the elements. But this was different. Back home, he would never have ventured outside in the nude.

Each new hardship was part of the training, he had been told. A few of the older pupils had warmed to him, albeit slightly, but it was enough for them to give him the little warning that it was this difficult for all of them in their first months. The Wampeh Ghalian were the most deadly killers in the galaxy, and beyond training, an aspirant's natural proclivities weighed heavily in their success in the trying profession.

Some contracts would require a strength of mind and will that simply went beyond what could be taught. And what better time to assess a pupil than when they were new and raw, their reactions and emotions unguarded?

Hozark had been standing, at attention, nude, in the chill for nearly an hour when one of the instructors came to fetch him.

"You are to come with me," the Ghalian said.

Hozark began to pick up his clothing.

"No. Leave those. Come as you are."

"But, it's cold, and I'm—"

The man's sharp look silenced the boy as effectively as the crack of a whip. Quietly, young Hozark followed the instructor. He had been subjected to more hardships in his short time there than his entire life on Arkanis. And it was only beginning.

All eyes fell upon him when he was ushered onto the dirt floor of the training chamber. The air was, he noted, at least slightly warmer, though that may have been because of the body temperature of the two dozen other pupils standing there quietly waiting for him. Not one of the boys or girls moved an inch, though a few glances were cast his way.

Naked. In front of the other students. It was embarrassing enough as is, but this was worse. There were *girls* present. Had he not been so cold, Hozark would have felt a blush rise to his cheeks. And it would only get worse. Today, he would be forced to fight nude. To grapple with boys and girls alike.

When her turn came, Samara gave a little grin, distracting him from his defensive posturing before flipping him to the ground. They were both too young to have begun the change into adults, but the taboo of their closeness was not lost on them.

Soon enough, though, he would learn to ignore those feelings entirely. No embarrassment. No interest. No fear. Modesty had no place on the battlefield, and the Wampeh Ghalian knew that better than most. That was why they trained the way they did. By the time those who possessed the strength of body and will had become full-fledged Wampeh Ghalian assassins, their prowess was unquestionable.

In fact, even naked, a fully trained Wampeh Ghalian could eliminate a roomful of armed soldiers, if they were forced to do so. It would likely come at a cost, but if there happened to be a power user present, their other ability would allow them to heal their wounds and carry on with their mission. It was an unlikely event, mind you, but it had happened in the past.

It was Master Garrusch, in fact, who had been captured, stripped, tortured, and prepared for execution in his younger days, and he still bore many scars from the ordeal. Not out of necessity, but as a reminder to not only himself, but the pupils he was teaching, that a Ghalian master does not *need* weapons to be deadly.

Every few years, the students of the various training houses across the many systems would get a visit from the older master, whereupon he would take all challengers in his demonstration of a master Ghalian's skill. And he would do it in the nude.

Those who thought themselves rather skilled would line up, attacking him individually, or, more often than not, en masse. It was no matter. His skills compared to even the senior-most instructors seemed almost otherworldly. The five masters were simply an order of magnitude more deadly than all but the highest-tier Ghalian. And each possessed their own unique style. For the young trainees, watching the demonstrations was like being afforded a glimpse of a talent they could all hope for but would never achieve.

All but a few, that is.

"Each of you will be assessed," Master Garrusch had told them after his demonstration, pacing the line of attentive students while he was still nude.

Modesty was the farthest thing from his mind, and he wore his body and his scars with an easy confidence.

"Your abilities have been noted and gauged since your arrival here, and your own personal style will be honed to a fine edge as your training progresses to the next levels," he continued. "While you will learn things that may not feel as comfortable or natural to the way you move or think, you must always remember that knowing the fighting styles of your enemies is of utmost importance to a Wampeh Ghalian."

It was a lesson that both Hozark and Samara had taken to heart, and the two of them would often train in obscure and difficult styles from the far reaches of the galaxy in their off hours. And as they grew older, they even incorporated minor elements that had once seemed so difficult and unnatural into their own personal styles as easily as breathing.

This degree of drive was what led them to excel. To rise rapidly through the ranks. And Master Garrusch, more than most, had expressed his satisfaction with their progress.

Then, one day, hushed word spread through the training house. Master Prombatz called a gathering of all students, teachers, and visiting Ghalian in the largest chamber.

"One of the Five has fallen," he announced to the gathered assassins. "Master Garrusch has completed his final contract."

Hozark and Samara shared a quick glance. None in the room would dare react aloud, but for many there, Garrusch was something of a personal mentor, and his loss, though expected for one in their line of work, was nonetheless a blow.

It was the closest Hozark ever came to seeing plain emotion on the others' faces as they processed the information. And had he been but a few years younger, he might have felt tears well up in his eyes. But he was older now. Almost a full member of the order. Emotions were a weakness they could not afford.

A few days later, the messengers from the various training houses and Ghalian estates had relayed their oral messages, as was the way of the order. And a day after that, a new member of the Five was chosen from the topmost ranks of their membership.

The transfer of power was quick, and it was simple. The Wampeh Ghalian were not ones for unnecessary pomp. Ghalian Varsuvala became *Master* Varsuvala, and that was that. She took up the position with all of the seriousness and pride in her work that was expected of the role.

As for the deceased Master Garrusch, his most powerful and valuable possessions were taken by one of the Three—those who held fast the secret location of the Wampeh Ghalian's most valuable treasures—to be placed in the hidden vault on a distant world.

The remaining magical items, such as his daily konuses and slaaps, were then added to the general stockpile for use by the others as need arose. One day, Hozark would even wear one of Garrusch's old konuses into battle. But that had been a long, long time away.

# CHAPTER NINE

Hozark flew in total silence as he mulled over the mission before him. Eliminating Visla Horvath would be no easy task under even the most ideal of circumstances. But he was protected, and by far more than some mere Tslavar mercenaries.

Samara was a skilled assassin. And on top of that, she possessed a blade of rather terrifying power. Corann had been correct in her assessment. If he was to succeed in this task, he, too, would need a vespus blade.

"Orkut. Where could you possibly be?" the pale man wondered, the legendary bladesmith's name the first sound to pass his lips since he'd taken his leave of the training house.

Only a very few knew the carefully protected means of producing the Wampeh Ghalian's most deadly of blades. A particular type of sword, its blue metal channeled and redirected the power a Ghalian absorbed, helping them better wield the stolen magic.

The spell bound to the metal, diverting the energy into its glowing blue length, was known to a mere handful. And those few kept that particular talent hidden. While their bladesmithing skills might be known to many, their value to the Wampeh Ghalian was a well-kept secret from all.

The master artisans were paid *very* well for their skills, and they were guaranteed protection without question. But even so, their numbers had shrunk over the years. And now, only a few remained. And of them, Orkut was by far the most skilled.

He was also the hardest to find. In fact, for all intents and purposes, he had ceased to exist. Of course, the Wampeh Ghalian knew better. The man was a recluse on the best of days, and with hostilities brewing within the Council of Twenty, his skills might well be called upon by more than the Ghalian. And so, Orkut had seemingly vanished.

But anyone can be found with enough time, coin, and patience. It wouldn't be easy, though.

The order had an impressive network of spies spread throughout most systems, and it was precisely those assets who helped Hozark obtain a number of solid leads as to the possible whereabouts of Orkut. But it would require a great deal of skill and finesse to narrow down the possible locations of the reclusive blacksmith further. And there was simply no way Hozark could do it alone.

"Hey, buddy! Didn't expect to be hearing from you again so soon," Uzabud said as Hozark pulled his personal ship up to the larger craft.

"Nor I, my friend, but it would appear I am in need of your services and expertise once more."

"Always glad to help out. You know that," Bud said. "So, what is it this time? Infiltrating a Barinjian battle group? Or sabotaging a fleet of Tslavar war craft? Ooh, ooh! Or snatching a princess from the clutches of an elderly arranged husband with poor hygiene?"

Hozark couldn't help but roll his eyes. "I will tell you when I am aboard, Bud. I can say this, though. It is something far less exciting, yet exponentially more difficult."

"Consider my interest piqued," Bud replied. "Can't wait to hear all about it. See ya in a few."

Hozark latched his ship to Bud's and secured it with a trio of fastening spells, then deployed his umbilical spell, the magical tube providing him oxygen and warmth as he walked from one ship to the other. Uzabud's new copilot was waiting for him when the door opened.

"Hey, it's really nice to see you again," Laskar said. "Uzabud wouldn't tell me what the new mission is. Just that we're going to be following your lead again. So, anything exciting?"

"As I told Uzabud, it will not be exciting, no. But it will certainly be a challenge."

"Excellent! I love a good challenge. I'll be a great help, no doubt," Laskar said with overabundant confidence.

The man was certainly enthusiastic, if nothing else, and, though Hozark still wasn't exactly fond of the cocky pilot, the extra set of eyes could prove most useful on this outing. Especially if things got rough. For Bud to vouch for his piloting skills said a lot about the man's talents. And this time around, if things went sideways, he just might get to show them off.

"Hey, Hozark," Bud said as the assassin walked into command with his copilot in tow. "So, you going to tell me what this is all about?"

"He says it's going to be a tough one."

"Yes, Laskar, I know that. You were with me when he called it in."

"I know. Just saying, is all."

Uzabud shook his head. "You've gotta trust me, the guy really does have a knack for this sort of thing. When he's not sticking his foot in his mouth, that is."

Hozark flashed a disarming smile. And more often than not it was precisely that which his grin preceded. The disarming of an enemy, and their subsequent slaughter. This time, however, his motives were far less violent.

"Of course, old friend. I understand. And from what Laskar has been saying, if he indeed has the piloting talents he professes, he may prove to be an increasingly useful acquisition to your crew."

"And I'm good in a scrape too!" the pilot noted.

"Seriously? What did we talk about? A little modesty wouldn't hurt, Laskar," Bud said with an exasperated sigh. "Anyway, what sort of thing did you have in mind, Hozark?"

The Wampeh paused a moment and looked at the two men. Yes, Bud was certainly up for the task. Laskar? Well, he was a bit annoying, and an unproven factor. But this was not a critical mission. At least not in the blow-up-and-die-if-you-fail way. So, if he could help find Orkut, great. If not, he would be living ballast. And Hozark had no problem lightening the load if need be.

"We are seeking out a particular individual," he said. "He will be difficult to locate. Well hidden."

"Was he kidnapped?" Laskar asked.

"No."

"Who is it?"

"His name is of no matter to you," the Wampeh replied. "Only that he is a master bladesmith. His location has been narrowed to a few dozen likely worlds. Our task is to further refine those and search for word of one of his talents on one of them. But if you must, you may refer to him as Master Tokro."

Hozark could have shared Orkut's real name, but as a bladesmith for the Wampeh Ghalian, anonymity was something of paramount importance. Tokro was the last pseudonym the swordmaker had used, and, unless things had gone so sideways for him that he found himself needing a new one, that name should still suffice in locating him on whichever world he was now hidden.

"What's the plan, then? You said a few dozen. That's a lot of space to cover. Especially if the systems are far apart. Jump magic can only take us so far, after all," Bud noted.

"I am well aware of that limitation, which is why we will begin with a preliminary survey of the nearest worlds while the Ghalian network seeks out more information for us."

The Wampeh pulled a list from inside his tunic. "These are the worlds you will be surveying. They are well within your usual area of operation, so your paid eyes should be able to tell you if he is there or not. Or at least give you an indication of where to look, if they don't know for sure."

Uzabud took the list and glanced at it once before handing it to Laskar.

"Easy hops, mostly," the copilot said, handing it back. "You want to split them up and save some time?"

"With Hozark's approval," Bud said.

The Wampeh nodded. "A wise use of resources. Begin your task immediately. I shall do likewise. We will then meet back at the rendezvous point noted on the list in seven days, unless you have a definite hit before then, in which case you will long-range skree me immediately."

"Sounds like a plan," Bud said. "C'mon, Lassie, let's prep for our first runs."

"I do wish you'd stop calling me that," Laskar grumbled.

"And if wishes were Malooki, beggars would eat steak," the former pirate replied with a laugh. "We'll see you in a few days, Hozark. And hopefully with good news."

"I share that hope," the Wampeh said, then headed back to his own ship. A minute later he had released his spells and was on his way, hopeful they might find Orkut without too much fuss. But deep in his gut, he knew that was going to be highly unlikely.

# CHAPTER TEN

It was during a careful survey of the sixth consecutive world the Ghalian operatives had scoped out, but with no success thus far, that Hozark's otherwise boring little adventure took an abrupt turn. At least it was *something*, although not what he was looking for.

Bud and Laskar were both out in other systems, scanning as best they could for any sign of the mysterious Orkut, leaving the Wampeh Ghalian to himself as he made his way to yet another world. And this one was a doozy.

Dropping down from orbit, Hozark found himself landing on a planet so verdant and alive with growth that it almost hurt the eye. As he drew closer and set the ship down, he noted something else. It was lush absolutely *everywhere*. And the world was crackling with magic.

Curious, Hozark cast the smallest of pushing spells at a nearby shrub. Nothing violent. Just enough to make it move from the force. But instead of simply rustling, as was the caster's intent, the shrub instead reacted in a most violent manner, puffing up its leaves and spraying out a burst of harmful retaliatory magic.

It seemed the system's red dwarf sun was emitting a particularly potent form of energy that imbued the native plant life with some rather disconcerting properties. Namely, when the wrong kind of magic was used near them, or, heaven forbid, against them, they would react, their innate defensive mechanisms engaging like a skunk, but of flora origin.

He was not sure if all the world's plants possessed this trait, but Hozark was in no mood to find out. Fending off magical deterrents was exhausting work, and this place was full of them, it seemed. It was also what made it a perfect place for Orkut to hide out.

There were few settlements in the dangerous landscape. Carving them out of the wilderness without killing those building them was difficult work. An arduous process that took decades, yet still cost many lives. Those who had survived, though, were a very, very hardy type, and as a result, only the toughest visited this world.

Again, a perfect hiding place for the powerful swordsmith seeking to be left alone.

Hozark had surveyed the smaller towns with some speed. As on the previous worlds, signs of Orkut would be easy enough to detect with his Ghalian senses. But so far it seemed he was coming up empty yet again. It was only in the largest of the rather dense cities that he felt the first hint of something. A bit of power, though he couldn't be sure if it was Orkut or something else.

He walked through the city with a leisurely gait, doing his best not to seem like anything more than another man out for a stroll. Being a master assassin, well versed in the art of subterfuge, he excelled at it. But sometimes, that just didn't matter.

The scent of magic was getting stronger. Not extremely powerful, but it was there. Hozark knew he was getting close to the source. He just hoped it was finally the man he sought.

As he homed in on the scent, a handful of large Tslavar mercenaries stepped out of the shadows shrouding the side alley of a squat building. A tavern of some sort, it seemed. Their muscles bulged within their green skin, and their body language was as aggressive as the looks in their eyes.

Hozark could handle them easily, of course, but the last thing he wanted was a scene. Not when he needed his target to remain calm. If Orkut caught wind of any danger, he might bolt, and tracking him down again would be even more difficult.

The assassin casually steered his course away from the approaching men. There were five of them, the smallest of the gang being the leader. It wasn't so much anything he said as it was the way he moved, and how the larger men around him followed his lead, like the Alpha of their little pack, that defined him.

And it was the Alpha who was matching his course.

"Excuse me," Hozark said, turning to confront the would-be attackers. "I'm new to this city and am seeking a local healer to help with my skin condition."

He had used variants of the ploy on several occasions. The visceral "eww, cooties" reaction the mention of skin disorders often elicited provided him the distance he needed to make a casual escape. But these men were different. They didn't seem to care about anything but their goal. Namely, his coin.

"Too bad for you, friend," the largest of the group said.

He was an imposing beast of a man, obviously chosen to take the lead in their shakedowns due to his sheer size. It was enough to intimidate just about anyone. Anyone who wasn't a Wampeh Ghalian, that is.

With the goons so close, Hozark was able to get a far better sense of the men.

*Damn,* he thought. The magic he'd sensed wasn't coming from Orkut. No, it was one of the thugs who possessed a modicum of power. He'd been taking it slow and careful for nothing, it seemed.

"Give us your coin and all of your belongings," the man continued. "Or I'll have to get rough."

"Oh, *you'll* get rough with *me*?" Hozark said, his sweet and calm demeanor sliding from him like water from an oily surface. "How quaint."

The would-be muggers looked at one another in confusion. This was not how it was supposed to go. The target should have been cowering in his boots, handing over his possessions in a panicked hurry. But instead, he was smiling at them. And there was *something* about that smile they all found quite unnerving but couldn't quite put their fingers on.

The smaller man took charge, trying to salvage the heist. "Grab him. Into the alley, quick!"

The goon seized the pale man by the arm and dragged him from the main street, as ordered.

It was precisely as Hozark had wanted. He would perhaps break the tiniest of sweats negating this pathetic threat, but he could at least top off his power from the magic user among them in the process.

The men felt something terribly wrong in the air but didn't know what it was. Uneasy, they closed in on their prey, just as he let the remainder of his disguise slip away as his fangs slid into place.

"A Ghalian!" the enormous man managed to squeak just moments before the assassin ended him. As he fell, the others realized just what a terrible mistake they had made and tried to flee. But it was far, far too late.

Hozark cast a silencing spell across the alleyway, blocking all sounds from escaping, the same fate as the men whose screams no one would be able to hear. The assassin dropped four of them in quick order, pausing to drain the meager magic from the fifth. He then used some of that power to cast a levitation spell and move the dead men to a nearby corral.

The sounds from within told him all he needed to know. This was a fortuitous turn of events that would save him wasting precious magic to get rid of the bodies.

The Bundabist within the corral were not dangerous creatures. In fact, they were quite harmless. But they were omnivores with sharp teeth and strong jaws, and they ate just about anything. He hefted the bodies into the enclosure, and the animals set to work with hungry gusto.

They would dispose of the remains in short order, leaving no trace of the violence that had just occurred. And Hozark would continue his quest, heading off for yet another world. He hoped Bud and Laskar had better luck than he had.

# CHAPTER ELEVEN

Quietly orbiting the uninhabited third moon circling the planet Iggnaz, Uzabud and Laskar were eating a hearty meal of roasted vegetables sourced from the little world below.

While both men were omnivores, as was pretty much anyone who often lived in space for any long periods, they each preferred lighter fare. But having limited edible resources in the systems they visited at times forced them to not be terribly picky eaters and take what they could get in the way of supplies. Fortunately, Iggnaz had been something of a boon for them. A pleasant surprise in a mission full of frustration and dead ends.

Neither had ever been to that system before, let alone that planet, and happening upon its abundant marketplaces had been a most welcome discovery. Laskar had arrived first and sourced a hearty supply of fresh produce. When Uzabud joined him a day later, his copilot docked his smaller vessel and helped restock the mothership's larder.

"This is fantastic," Uzabud said between mouthfuls of a savory-sweet variety of root vegetable.

"I know, right?" Laskar said. "I could get used to this. I mean,

I know we have a bunch more systems to search, but maybe we could stay here just a bit longer."

Uzabud flashed a knowing look. "Trust me when I tell you this. When Hozark is on a mission, *nothing* will keep him from his goal. Not injury, not exhaustion, not hot or cold. And certainly not something as pedestrian as food. Why, one time, while stalking a target for weeks and weeks, he ran out of supplies, but that didn't stop him. He stayed in position and ate three rotten Malooki while lying quietly in wait."

"It was *two*," a voice said.

Uzabud and Laskar leapt to their feet, weapons ready. Hozark laughed and shed his shimmer cloak.

"And they were only Bundabist, not Malooki," he said of the horse-like creatures. "Look at the size of me, Uzabud. Do you really think I could eat an entire Malooki, let alone three?"

"Well, it makes for a better story," Bud replied, relaxing his pull on his konus's magic and sheathing his blade.

Laskar, however, held his at the ready a moment longer before following suit, eyes still wide at the man's sudden appearance.

"How did you do that? We didn't see any trace of you or your ship. And I set the wards and alarms myself. I know they were in place."

"He's a master Ghalian, Laskar," Uzabud replied for his friend. "Trust me, if he doesn't want to be seen, he won't be. All but the most powerful of vislas wouldn't stand a chance."

Laskar sat back down, but now only picked at the food before him. Having someone sneak up on them like that, aboard their own ship, no less, was more than a little disconcerting.

"Apologies, Laskar," Hozark said. "I did not intend to frighten you and put you off your meal."

"I wasn't frightened," the man blustered, digging back into his food, but with less gusto than previously.

Hozark and Uzabud shared a little glance and a grin.

"Of course not," Hozark said. "In any case, as you did not send a long-range skree, but rather came to the rendezvous point, I assume you had as little success in your efforts as I did."

"Unfortunately, that's the case," Bud replied. "Neither of us found a thing. Not even a whisper of the guy."

"Yeah, he's like a ghost," the copilot mumbled through his full mouth, dribbling a piece onto the table.

"Charming, Laskar," Bud joked.

Hozark raised a brow. "A geist, you say? Perhaps not. But he is definitely a capable man, and one who has apparently proving far more difficult to trace than our network gave him credit for."

"So, what do we do?" Bud asked.

"There are over a dozen more worlds to go, but I think we've learned our lesson. Given these results, we are just going to cut straight to the chase," Hozark said.

Laskar swallowed hard, nearly choking himself in the process. "You mean—?"

"Yes," the assassin replied. "We are going to Xymotz."

"Awww shit," Bud grumbled. "Here we go."


Xymotz. It was a somewhat notorious planet among scavengers, pirates, mercenaries, and other less-than-savory sorts. Naturally, Bud knew of it. He'd avoided it all these many years and never particularly wanted to pay a visit. Unfortunately, that didn't seem to be an option any more.

It was a place whose dangers were far greater than merely the rough and ready folk on its surface. Xymotz was a gas giant at the farther edges of its system, where it orbited a yellow dwarf star that only emitted a fairly minimal stream of power, and a variety useless to most.

The planet, though gaseous in nature, actually possessed a

small, solid orb at the center of the dense, poisonous clouds that comprised nearly all of its mass. Normally, the crushing gravity found on the surface would have prevented any life whatsoever from making a foothold there, but centuries upon centuries of magic had been layered upon the inhabited section, creating a sort of eddy in the swirling river of death.

Some might think the place an easy target for raiders seeking a new hideout. And they'd be right, if not for one important detail. Namely, the only means of arrival and departure was a single, narrow funnel of magic weaving through the deadly clouds.

It was the only way in and also the only means of escape. Something Bud was not happy about one bit. The perfect place for a trap, and being trapped was not something he was particularly fond of. Though it was for precisely that reason people were sure to behave on the surface, he was nevertheless not thrilled about the prospect. Fortunately, Hozark had given him an easy out.

"I want you and Laskar to stand lookout from orbit, safely outside the disruptive forces of the planet's clouds," the Wampeh said as they completed the final jump to the system.

"Don't have to tell me twice," Bud replied, settling the ship into orbit.

"Really?" Laskar said. "You say he's good, sure, but is it smart to go in alone?"

Bud winced at the man's tone. If he wasn't such a talented pilot, he just might have left him at the next world. Blurting things like that to one of the deadliest men in the galaxy—and his friend, no less—could wear one's welcome thin, and quickly.

"I shall be fine," Hozark said. "And if I should not be, you will report my demise to the others."

"Of course," Bud replied. "But let's not go that route just yet."

"It is not my intention, my friend."

The Ghalian assassin strolled to his shimmer ship and

boarded it. He did not need to bring any supplies from the mothership. A Ghalian always had what he needed at hand. Minutes later, he released the magical clamps holding him on Bud's ship and drifted away, engaging his Drookonus and powering up his own magical propulsion system.

"I'm going in," he said over his skree. "Should any threat appear, I shall have my long-range skree on my person at all times. Hopefully its power will cut through the interference."

"Gotcha," Bud replied. "We'll be ready up here with our eyes open." He then settled into a comfortable position with the dozen or so other ships lingering near the funnel accessway's gaping maw.

No one wanted to come up blind into a firefight or trap, and, thus, each was on guard, providing a similar service for their envoys to the planet below.

"Can you still hear me, Bud?" Hozark queried over the long-range skree as he passed the halfway mark.

"Yeah, I hear you. But your message is a bit fuzzy. This planet is wreaking merry havoc with your skree."

"So it would seem," Hozark said. "The magic in the clouds, as well as the planet's own gravity well are indeed something to behold. I will save the skree's power and only contact you in case of emergency from this point on. Until later, my friend."

"Safe travels," Bud replied.

"Safe? This place is anything but safe," Laskar pointed out.

He was right. The top half of the magical funnel was dangerous, but survivable. But Hozark had just reached the midway point. There, the heat generated by the density of the gasses was not quite enough to form a second sun in the solar system, but it was certainly enough to melt any manner of ship that ventured outside the narrow tube of magical protections.

The sheer amount of power that had been poured into fixing them in place was impressive to behold. Generations of visitors and inhabitants alike had added their own contributions as they could, reinforcing and buttressing the spells, keeping the layered protections from collapsing and crushing all within to oblivion. The center of it all was like a tiny bubble of safety clinging to the edge of a churning whirlpool of death.

And Hozark was flying right into it.

# CHAPTER TWELVE

The surface of Xymotz was far more hospitable than Hozark would have expected of such an unusual world. Rough edifices and unbearable climate were logical, given what he knew of the place, but, instead, the surface was quite peaceful. Peaceful, and clean where one expected anything but.

It seemed that the magic used to support the funnel was only a small portion of the protective spells layered upon the hidden civilization, and the bulk of them––the hardiest, at least––were reserved for the surface dwellers' comfort and quality of life.

"Fascinating," the Wampeh mumbled as he stepped from his ship and strode into the quaint, yet relatively spread out city.

It took up far more space than he would have expected, to be honest. Underground dwellings would make sense, given harsh environs, but with the tranquil skies within the magical bubble, there had simply been no such need, and buildings climbed up several stories as a result.

There were some subterranean fabrications, naturally, but it seemed as if they were mostly used for storage rather than habitation.

Hozark sniffed the air, not with his nose, but with his Wampeh Ghalian senses.

"Yes, a trace," he noted with a little smile. "And this time, I think I know who the owner is." He pulled his skree from his belt. "Uzabud, if you can hear this, I have reached the surface safely and am en route toward what may very well be our target. I will check back in with you later. If you do not hear from me in three days, assume me dead."

It was a morbid thing to say, but he'd run with the former pirate a long time, and they both knew full well that their demise was always a possibility on any mission. Even the seemingly easy ones. You just never knew.

It would be a stealthy hunt, but not his most difficult. Orkut was of particularly notable appearance, his race possessing a deep violet skin color far darker than the light violet of some of the residents of Slafara and other Council worlds. So dark it bordered on actual purple among some of his kind. Compared to the other inhabitants of this world, he would stand out. Yes, finding the swordsmith should be at least somewhat easy. That is, if he was there in the first place.

But the people of Xymotz were a tight-lipped bunch, and it took several hours of cajoling and buying rounds of drinks, all under the guise of Alasnib the trader—one of Hozark's favorite personas for this sort of infiltration and intelligence gathering operation—before he managed to learn the likely whereabouts of the one man fitting that description.

Of course, the drunk had not told him so outright. Even inebriated, which took quite a lot for the hard-drinking locals, they were a cautious bunch. Even the smallest nuggets of information were only gleaned by careful listening rather than outright spilling of details.

Fortunately, Alasnib, while a heavy drinker himself, was also protected by a most unusual spell. One that displaced whatever went into the caster's mouth and deposited it some hundred meters away. It might have seemed odd to any bystanders who witnessed alcohol appearing out of thin air down the road, but for Hozark, this little trick allowed him to match shots with his new friends, yet remain entirely cold sober, though he appeared to be anything but.

"Thass enufff," the Wampeh slurred as he unsteadily rose to his feet, swaying like a reed in the breeze. "I've gotta pishhh."

"Hurry back. We'll watch yer drinksh for ya," one of his sloshed companions said with a thick tongue and bloodshot eyes.

Hozark stumbled through the doors and out onto the street, where he made a weaving path toward a dark side alley. Once there, he slumped against the wall, carefully taking in his surroundings and ensuring none were watching. With the coast clear, he shifted his attire, shed the disguise, and carried on toward his destination under a new persona. A sober one, at that.

The building he'd been steered to was a squat structure near the waste processing area set out at the edge of town. The smell was surprisingly foul the closer he approached. Normally, that would be expected, but with all of the magic at work, there was simply no way the casters would have overlooked so simple and minor a thing to remedy with their years upon years of castings.

No. This was intentional. Someone was making the area unappealing for a reason. And he had a very good idea whom that someone was.

The doorway seemed a straightforward enough affair. A set of two slabs with worn pads for one's hand that pivoted them inward easily with a push, revealing a five-meter-long hallway with a pair of glowing sconces on each wall. Hozark was about to step inside when he paused, his Ghalian senses tingling. Carefully, he stepped back, studying the pattern on the floor. Red rune lines were faintly raised from the surface of the tiles.

"Clever," the assassin said with an appreciative grin, then

pulled the doors closed from the outside. He then applied a gripping spell to the push panels and pulled the doors open rather than push.

They hesitated a moment, then swung outward. And the raised runes embedded in the tiles were no longer visible. A misdirect trap, it seemed. And one that was mechanical in nature. Open the doors the wrong way and you would fall victim to the magical runes once you stepped inside, the passageway leading you to the normal-seeming, yet incorrect, corridor. Open them the correct way, however, and you had free passage to an otherwise hidden passage.

The Wampeh stepped inside and closed the doors behind him, moving carefully to the end of the hallway where the newly revealed door lay. If the first ward was any indication, this might take a while, and it would require all of his attention.

The interior of the building was warm. Warmer than would be expected for such thick walls. Then he noted the slight decline of the path he was following. He was descending, heading deeper beneath the surface, where the protective spells were the strongest. The heat from the planet's core was seeping through, it seemed, but nothing deadly. At least not yet. Not from the planet itself, anyway.

A trio of deadly magical wards threatened to separate his head from his body as he moved past a low-hanging tapestry. Yet another trap, and one that sent him diving and rolling out of the way of the cascading magic until he arrived at a seemingly safe spot at the center of the chamber he'd taken shelter in.

But it could not be so simple.

The heavy stones of the floor began falling away, dropping dozens of meters to a pit below. But they didn't crash on the bottom, Hozark noted as he raced across the portion of the floor that had stayed intact. There was a narrow, but passable path to the far doorway, should he but make a dash for it.

But something held him back. A glimpse of extra darkness in the murky depth at his feet.

He squinted his sharp eyes and focused hard. Yes, there was something down there. And more than that, there were *several* somethings. Stones, it seemed, and darker than the ones from the floor above. So dark as to be nearly invisible to the naked eye. Again, the Wampeh smiled in appreciation.

"*Very* well done," he said with an approving nod as he jumped not across to the pathway out, but *down* to the hidden stepping stones below.

It was a long way down, and the descent tested his reflexes to the max, but Hozark was sure of foot, and in short order had scampered across the stones to the well-hidden passageway's dark entrance.

The smell of magic was stronger here, he noted. But he refrained from striding into the corridor in a victorious rush. No, that would be the undoing of many, he suspected. But Hozark was not many. He was a Wampeh Ghalian, and one of the Five, at that. He paused and reached out with his senses, not for the obvious magic around him, but, rather, for the hidden.

"Ah, yes. There it is," he mused as a faint tickle caught his attention. "Masterful."

Hozark stepped forward to the threshold of the passage but paused. Eyes closed, he reached out with his left hand, his senses guiding it to a slender gap between the stones in the wall. He slid his index finger inside and depressed the magical release lever.

Lights flooded the chamber as the fallen stones soared back to their original location far above and the treacherous floor transformed into a smooth and safe expanse of immaculate tile.

Hozark turned and looked across the now illuminated room. He felt the eyes on him before he'd even turned, of course, but he knew better than to spin suddenly. To do so would be rude in this person's house.

A short man with wrinkled, deep-violet skin stood at the far end of the room, smiling at him with dancing golden eyes. Now that he was no longer masking his presence, Hozark could feel the power wafting off of the ancient man. He was far older and far more powerful than expected. But he possessed something far greater than mere magic. Something his birthright could not afford him.

The knowledge and skill acquired with years upon years of hard work.

And given his elderly appearance, and that in *spite* of his magic, Hozark guessed the man had been at it a very, very long time.

# CHAPTER THIRTEEN

"Master Orkut," the Wampeh said as he strode slowly to the middle of the chamber and kneeled, bowing his head, exposing the nape of his neck as he did so.

It was an utterly *wrong* thing to do in any remotely hostile situation. And for a Wampeh Ghalian, one who had the opposite drilled into him since his youth, it felt even more so. Hozark couldn't remember the last time he was so vulnerable. Yet, for this man's services, he must humble himself. He had come seeking the greatest of the Ghalian-affiliated swordmiths still living, and this was simply the way it had to be done.

Orkut said nothing, merely stepping forward on short legs, slowly walking to the kneeling man. Hozark was much taller than he, yet kneeling like this, they were now on somewhat even footing. That didn't mean it was not still dangerous for the assassin.

Yes, he had proven his worth by successfully passing the myriad wards and traps protecting the building and the man housed inside, but now there was one final test.

The blade maker himself would judge him. And only if he

was found truly worthy would he even consider taking up the challenge of making a new vespus blade.

The violet-skinned man stopped in front of the kneeling Wampeh and reached out with his right hand. His crafting hand. His *power* hand, for his kind channeled their energies in a circular, flowing manner within their bodies. Left hand for healing, right hand for power. And sometimes, death.

Orkut gently placed his hand on Hozark's exposed neck, running it along the length from his shoulders to his hairline. The assassin marveled at just how hot the man's palm felt on his skin, unlike so many elderly whose touch was cold, as if they were already halfway into the grave.

The swordsmith unexpectedly pricked his skin with a nail, drawing a small drop of blood, yet the Wampeh did not flinch. The master craftsman uttered a whispered spell as he studied the blood. A moment later he smiled.

"You may rise, Hozark of the Wampeh Ghalian," the man said.

"Thank you, Orkut," he replied. "Your tests were very well thought out. Challenging. Elegant in their design and execution. You have my deepest respect for your skills."

"Oh, you need not flatter an old man, Wampeh. I know my skills and do not need my ego stroked."

"I assure you, that was not my intent. Merely to state appreciation for your work."

"Hmm," was all the shorter man said, and that with a little grunt. "Hands."

Hozark held them out. Orkut took the assassin's hands in his own and turned them over, studying every inch of them, all the way to the elbows, with the eyes of an expert before letting them fall back to his sides.

"A vespus blade, eh?"

"I would not seek you out in your home otherwise."

"And you know what it is you ask of me?"

"Yes. And I am prepared to pay your price, whatever it is. The Wampeh Ghalian always make good on our debts, and my word is not only my bond, but that of my order."

"Oh, I'm quite aware of that," the swordsmith replied with an amused little grin. He then stood still and stared at the man before him.

Hozark had years and years of experience ignoring the scrutiny of others. It was what had made him such a talented infiltrator and efficient killer. But something about the way the man was looking at him made him almost shift and fidget with discomfort. *Almost.* He was a master for a reason, and controlling his emotions and impulses was a vital part of it.

Again, Orkut smiled, and the sensation lessened.

*Ah, another test, I see,* Hozark realized. The silence, however, continued.

"What do you need of me to begin, Master Orkut?" he finally asked, unsure if he was doing the right thing by speaking.

"Nothing."

"Nothing?"

"That's what I said," the blade maker replied. "I observed you this whole time. How you moved as you approached my home. How you moved when in disguise plying the townsfolk with drinks."

"You were there? How did I not see you?"

"I have my ways," the elderly man said with a mischievous twinkle in his eye. "And I watched how you maneuvered your way through my wards and booby traps. Yes, I know you quite well now, I think. Well enough to craft you a most deadly blade. One that once in your hands will move as if a part of your body itself."

Hozark couldn't help but appreciate the man's talents. He had not only seen him coming long before the assassin had even sensed his magic, but he had also crafted his traps and diversions with a second, ulterior motive in mind. A two-fold purpose for his tests.

Any who would wield a vespus blade would have to possess great skill, but to have one crafted new, especially for them, well, that simply wasn't done anymore. They were always handed down from teacher to pupil, or inherited upon the demise of another. But this was different. His would be a blade forged specifically for Hozark. And the master craftsman had studied him well.

Hozark reached to his waist for the heavy pouch of coin. "I have the payment in full, as is customary," he said.

"Stop," Orkut replied, fixing his golden gaze upon the Wampeh once more. "I have heard that you now fight the Council of Twenty."

"You know the Wampeh Ghalian do not take sides."

"No, of course not," Orkut said in his least convincing tone. "And I also hear that you seek to eliminate Visla Horvath."

"How did you know--?"

"I have not reached my current age without making more than a few friends of my own," Orkut replied. "With Emmik Rostall gone--your handiwork, I assume?"

Hozark nodded.

"As I thought. With him gone, and Visla Tumertz stepping in to fill his shoes, Visla Horvath is preparing to expand his influence, and greatly at that. The Council has always been a thorn in the side of free men, but these times are becoming even more dangerous. Greed and lust for power is threatening all but the most stable of systems. This chaos they are causing is even threatening my own home and those I hold dear."

"But none would dare attack Xymotz."

"No, dear Wampeh. I mean my *home*. The place I am from, but can never return to, lest I put my heirs at risk."

"I was unaware you had any."

"And that was intentional," the swordsmith replied. "But I am old, and someday my line will take up my mantle."

"They possess your gift? Your power?"

"My youngest does, yes. And I've trained him well." He fixed his eyes firmly on Hozark's. "I tell you this in confidence, Hozark of the Wampeh Ghalian, and I expect you to keep this secret until my demise. Until then, he is safe. And if no Ghalian requires another vespus blade, then it is my hope my youngest may live his life quietly, and without fear of the Council learning his true skill."

"Your secret is safe with me. You have my solemn word and vow. On my blood and the blood of my line."

Orkut nodded once. "Your mission aligns with my own desires, Wampeh. Put away your coin. Kill Visla Horvath and stop the Council's spread, and that is payment enough."

"Thank you, Master Orkut."

The violet man quietly uttered a portal spell, opening a small, magical path to the surface. The amount of power such a spell required was incredible, and for him to have cast it so easily, he must have been sitting on a wealth of Ootaki hair or some similar power store to do so. But Hozark knew better than to inquire.

"And the sword?" Hozark asked.

"You may return to your vessel. Inform your orbiting friends to standby a little longer. And in the meantime, go see the sights if you wish, what few there are on this rock. Or don't. The choice is yours. In any case, your sword will be ready in three days."

Hozark bowed deeply before the swordsmith, who replied with a little nod of his head, then strode through the portal back to the surface. All there was to do now was wait. And waiting was something he was an expert at.

# CHAPTER FOURTEEN

Orkut was as punctual as he was skilled at his craft, and precisely three days later to the very hour the agreement was made, a heavyset woman in a long cloak arrived at Hozark's parked craft.

The Wampeh was waiting nearby, watching her arrival from the safety of his shimmer cloak. It was not that he didn't trust Orkut. He did, and with his life, if need be. But caution was the Ghalian way, and he was going to be absolutely sure none had followed the courier. And, so far as he could tell, none had.

"I'm here with your delivery," the woman said into the ship's apparently open door.

She called out, but she did not step inside. A wise choice, as there was only a single warning spell in place before the more aggressive wards would kick in. The woman's voice was pleasant, and somewhat low in register. From what he could hear, Hozark thought she must be about thirty or so, though sounds could be deceiving. But there was something else about her. A whiff of power. And very, very familiar at that.

"From which training house?" Hozark asked, walking toward her after first shedding his shimmer cloak.

The woman turned with an utterly unsurprised look on her pale face.

"I thought you might be nearby," she said calmly, her pointed canines shining through her grin. A Wampeh. And a Wampeh Ghalian, at that. This was a sister of the order bearing his weapon. "It is a pleasure to see you, Master Hozark. You likely do not remember me. It has been many years since you visited the training house on——

"Oobanta," he replied with a hint of a grin of his own. "You trained on Oobanta, under Master Tiskan."

"Yes. Before he fell."

"A great loss to the Ghalian," Hozark said. "Though he lived a long and productive life. You were in Teacher Galdoh's cadre, were you not? Demelza, if I recall correctly."

"I was," she replied. "You remember me?"

"I remember those worth noting. And you most certainly had potential. A talented caster, as I recall. Tiskan spoke highly of your abilities. I was pleased when I learned you had successfully completed your training and became a full-fledged sister in the order."

Demelza was a Wampeh Ghalian, and her emotions were entirely under control. But in that moment, just for a split second, she could almost feel a flush threaten to rise to her cheeks. Praise from not only Master Tiskan, but Master Hozark as well? It was enough to fluster a lesser woman.

The weight in her hands suddenly garnered her attention. Dropping to one knee, she held out the carefully wrapped oilskin package to its new owner. Whatever it was, it was surprisingly light for its length and shape.

Hozark stepped forward and gently took the sword from her and began undoing the bindings. He paused, sensing the magic in his hands, and smiled.

"Oh, Orkut. You outdo yourself," he said appreciatively, then muttered a series of disarming spells.

It seemed the master swordsmith had taken precautions that only the sword's intended owner would sense. On the surface, there was no trace of the wrappings' true contents. And should any other foolishly attempt to claim its contents for their own, there were more than a few deadly wards in place on the innocuous-looking parcel.

Hozark reached out once more, taking great care to ensure he had removed *all* of the protections Orkut had put in place. Satisfied it was safe, he untied the formerly warded ties holding the oilcloth in place. The material fell away, revealing the first vespus blade forged by Orkut's hands in longer than any could remember.

He still produced weapons of exquisite design and deadly power, and those enchanted blades were sought out across the systems. But this? *This* was magnitudes stronger.

Demelza's eyes widened at the sight of the faintly glowing blue metal.

"A *vespus blade*?" she gasped. "I did not realize Orkut possessed this degree of skill."

"Yet you are here, in his employ. And delivering a vespus blade for him, I might add, which is an unusual thing in and of itself. How, exactly, is it that you, a Ghalian, are serving him? And on this world, of all places?"

"I spent a great deal of time pursuing whispers of the man," she replied. "Eventually, after a very long time, they brought me here. I sought him out with hopes of engaging him to craft a sword for me."

"And you managed to find him without the order's network? Most impressive," Hozark said.

"Perhaps. But I failed to pass all of his tests," Demelza admitted. "He spared me, though. Credit given for locating him in the first place, I suppose, as well as for the many of his traps and wards I *did* manage to evade. He would not do as I wished, however. But, upon reflection, he made me an offer."

"Oh? What sort of offer might he offer a Wampeh Ghalian, I wonder."

"A reasonable one, in my mind. He said that if I wished to eventually possess a blade forged by his hands, I must serve him when not on Ghalian business."

"And you are doing so now, I see."

"Whatever it takes to remain in his good graces," she replied, her eyes lingering on the newly forged blade.

Hozark muttered a tiny spell, directing a tiny portion of his cached power into the vespus blade's greedy length. The sword flashed bright blue, the magic crackling within. It was a particular weapon. One only the Wampeh Ghalian could wield to its true potential.

Yes, if captured, another could still use it as a blade, and it would be quite good at that job. But to channel power like this, only a Ghalian's hands could impart that final touch to activate its true potential.

It was more than a mere enchanted blade. It was a magical repository, storing and channeling the additional power a Wampeh Ghalian might drain from a victim. The magic would be held in the blade, accessible by a Ghalian, but no other. And in the possession of one such as Hozark, the strength of the sword would only grow.

In fact, once it had fully linked with its owner, the sword could hold enough magical potential that it could cut an enemy's limb clean off by simply being dropped on them.

The master assassin swung the vespus blade in a series of moves that were so ingrained it was as easy as breathing. Breathing. The very act the flowing motions would bring to a halt in whoever got in his way.

Hozark smiled so broadly, the joy even reached his eyes. It was *perfect*. Orkut had spoken true. The blade truly did feel as if it had always been in his hand. A part of him, as natural to wield as his own limbs. Properly maintained, it would remain as deadly as new for generations.

"Master Orkut has truly outdone himself," Hozark said.

Demelza was watching him with quiet respect.

"Would you like to hold it?" he asked, extending the blade to her, grip first.

"Thank you, Master Hozark," she said, reining in her glee as she felt the weapon's potential as it settled into her palm.

"Have you never before seen a vespus blade?" Hozark asked.

"Only once, but from a distance. A woman I had not seen before visited my training house. But it was sheathed, and her stay was brief. I never saw its full glory."

"Yes, that was one of the few remaining vespus blades in the order's possession," Hozark said, knowing in his gut it was Samara of whom she spoke. His stomach twisted slightly, but his face did not betray the flash of emotion within him.

Demelza nevertheless sensed the subtle shift in the man's mood and promptly handed the weapon back to him. "Thank you, Master Hozark. It is a beautiful blade."

"Thank you. We will cross paths again one day, you and I. Until then, I wish you the best of fortunes with Master Orkut. His skills are unrivaled."

"Indeed. And your sword is the acme of that knowledge. I know it will serve you well in our mission."

Hozark paused. "*Our* mission? Did you say *our* mission?"

"Didn't he tell you?"

"Tell me what?" he asked, a slight sinking feeling in his gut.

"Master Orkut was quite clear in his directions. He said I am to assist you in all ways possible to hinder the Council of Twenty and their plans, and to ensure the successful elimination of Visla Horvath."

Hozark worked alone. All Wampeh Ghalian did, and Orkut was well aware of that fact. Bud didn't count. He was a friend, certainly, but also a tool to be used in furthering his goals. Not a

78

Ghalian. Not one of the order. And after losing Enok so recently, the thought of bringing another young Ghalian into harm's way alongside him was distasteful.

But the master blade maker had just crafted perhaps his finest work, and for no charge. They shared similar goals, and this mission meant more to him than mere coin. Much as he wished to, Hozark knew better than to protest. He owed the man.

"It will be my pleasure having your assistance," he said. Demelza would perhaps be able to provide some help, and in the process, she would earn points with the violet-skinned man toward having her own weapon crafted. "Gather your things. We shall depart when you return."

"I already have them prepared," she replied.

"A sister Ghalian. Of course you do."

"I will retrieve them and be aboard in five minutes."

Hozark nodded. "Very well. Once we are safely aboard our mothership, I will introduce you to Bud and his new copilot. And then we begin our deadly work in earnest."

## CHAPTER FIFTEEN

"*Two* Wampeh Ghalian?"

"Yes, Bud."

"We've got *two* super-deadly assassins on our side now?" he said with glee.

"Yes, Bud," Hozark repeated.

Their overly enthused copilot had also perked right up when he learned Demelza would be joining them. "Oh, this Horvath fella is so screwed," Laskar added with a chuckle.

Hozark was not amused. "While I appreciate your confidence, you should not become any cockier than you already are," he said with a hint of annoyance. "This is a dangerous man. A *very* dangerous one. A visla, no less."

"Well, yeah. But you said he wasn't a super powerful one."

"Laskar, *any* visla is powerful. More than a mere emmik. You know this," Hozark replied. "He possesses the power to end any of us, if we are anything less than careful."

"So we don't screw up," Laskar replied. "I mean, how hard can it be? We fly in, do the job, then fly out. Simple."

Hozark glanced at Uzabud. His friend shared the pained expression. Laskar was a good pilot. Great, even. But his fearless, cocky attitude could very well be his demise. That was actually fine with the assassin, but he had no desire for his companions or himself to go down with him.

"If he engages us directly, it will be shocking if we come out on top. Stealth is the only way," the Wampeh said.

"I agree with Master Hozark," Demelza added. "Horvath will be quite a handful if he is aware of our approach."

"Demelza is right," Hozark said. "And the visla is protected."

"We can handle guards," Laskar said with a confident laugh.

Hozark looked at the crew. His friend. His Ghalian comrade. His obnoxious pilot. It was time to tell them the rest.

"He is protected by more than guards," he began.

"What, he's got Tslavar mercenaries?" Laskar joked. "Or Uvallian guard beasts? No problem."

"Actually, he does have mercenaries in his employ," the Ghalian master replied. "And, supposedly, some animal protection as well. But no, they are not my true concern. What is far more of a threat is his personal guard."

"Like I said, we can take—"

"He is protected by a Wampeh Ghalian," Hozark said.

It felt as if the air suddenly went out of the chamber as his words hit the other three like an arrow to a bull's eye.

"Did you say a Wampeh Ghalian?" Uzabud asked. "I could have sworn you just said Wampeh Ghalian."

"I did, Bud."

"A full-fledged member of the order?"

"Yes, Bud."

The jovial man paled. "But, how? Your kind don't do that sort of thing. Not ever. Demelza, back me up, here. I'm right, right?"

"You are, Uzabud. It is not a commission the Wampeh Ghalian ever accept."

Hozark sighed. "She is no longer a member of the order."

"She? So you know who she is?" Laskar asked.

Hozark sighed again. "Her name is Samara."

Demelza nearly gasped. "Samara? You mean Samara the Eviscerator?"

"Just Samara, please," Hozark said.

"Eviscerator?" Laskar asked. "Uh, why is she called that?"

Bud flashed his copilot a look. "You can't figure it out?"

"Well, yeah. But, I mean––"

"Because she would send a message with her target's remains, on occasion. Yes," Hozark said. "But, again, just Samara, please."

The pirate and his companion fell silent as they contemplated this new wrinkle in the plan. To face a visla was one thing, but one guarded by a Wampeh Ghalian––and a legendary one at that––was a whole new complication.

"I know stories of her," Demelza said. "She was quite prolific, from what I've heard. And one of our best."

"She was," the Ghalian agreed.

"And, didn't the two of you train together in the same house?"

Hozark hid it well, and his external demeanor showed nothing of the turmoil rolling inside of him. But despite his calm face, his very world was in turmoil. "Yes, we did. We trained together since we were children."

"So, you know her weaknesses, then," Laskar said.

"Some. But she has been gone a long time. There is no telling what new tricks she might have learned," Hozark replied.

Bud ran his hand though his hair in thought. "But you once said none ever leave the order. You said it's just not the sort of thing that's allowed."

"And it isn't. However, we thought her dead. Killed on a contract gone wrong, her remains strewn among the stars."

"But that's obviously not the case."

"No, it is not. And there is more. She possessed one of the last vespus blades when we believed her slain."

"Wait, the woman I saw in my training house? *That* was *Samara the Evis*—sorry, I mean, just, Samara?"

"Yes, Demelza. One and the same. And as you have likely deduced, in all likelihood, she is still in possession of that weapon."

The Ghalian woman nodded her head, the pieces all sliding into place. "Hence your visit to Orkut."

"Yes."

"You needed him to forge a vespus blade of your own if you were to face her."

"Yes."

"But the order doesn't have any stored with the weapons in the secret va—"

"No, they do not," he cut her off.

Bud and Laskar didn't say anything, but for a just a moment, Hozark thought he saw the briefest flash of curiosity in the copilot's eyes. Curiosity about Ghalian secrets never turned out well for those who went digging.

He would need to have a few private words with the man when the opportunity presented itself, and gently dissuade him from pursuing whatever wild idea was in his head any further. copilots, no matter how skilled, were of no use if they were dead, after all.

"So, things just got a whole lot more difficult," Bud grumbled. "It's going to be straight-up Ghalian-vs-Ghalian mayhem out there. I tell ya, I would sell tickets to the event, if we weren't all likely going to die in the process."

"Your vote of confidence is appreciated, old friend," Hozark said with a grim chuckle.

Laskar, however, was a bit less amused than before. "How in the worlds do we get past her?"

"Leave that to me."

"Fine. But where are we even going? You said it was a cold world. Which one? There are literally thousands of them."

"We are traveling to Arkanis," the assassin informed him. "And yes, it is a very cold world. Cold, and dark."

"Just lovely," Bud griped. "Is there any *good* news you'd care to share with us?"

Hozark flashed an amused look at his friend. "Well, there is one bit of news you have not yet heard."

"Oh? And what would that be?" Uzabud asked, suspiciously.

"Our spies have informed us that Visla Horvath is not always guarded by Samara."

"Thank the gods."

"He is also guarded by something else. Something quite deadly, from what they were able to ascertain."

"That's just great," Bud said with a sigh. "So, what is it, then?"

"They were unable to find out," Hozark replied. "But rest assured, my friend. We will learn what soon enough."

# CHAPTER SIXTEEN

Arkanis.

It was as shitty and cold as Hozark had remembered it. Despite being taken at a young age, he was mildly surprised to find his youthful recollections of the world to have been fairly accurate and not biased by his hardships. The young mind often embellished, but that was not so in this case.

The cold was just as biting. The darkness just as oppressive. As he exited his cloaked craft and stepped out onto the untouched snow, the crunch of that particular planet's frozen covering beneath his feet sent through him a rush of memories. Not all of them good. But in retrospect, one was.

Fahbahl had taken him from his home, and though it had been a tough life, it was all he had known at the time. But Hozark had been noticed. His particularly rare breed of magical potential had been identified and brought to the attention of the Wampeh Ghalian. And because of it, he had become the man he now was.

Mind you, he had no idea his life would be as rewarding and full as it was when he was bundled up and swept away from

Arkanis, but as an adult, he gave silent thanks to Fahbahl for what he had done all of those years ago.

Back home once more, his ship rested on a light cushion of magic just above the small patch of pristine snow covering the little field he had settled into a low hover above. With its shimmer engaged, it would remain invisible unless someone walked right up to it. The footprints he and his friends left behind, however, would require a little magic to erase.

"Hurry up," Uzabud called back to Laskar as he hopped out of the ship. "I want to get out of the cold sooner than later."

"I'm coming. Jeez," Laskar griped as he stepped out into the brisk air. "Sure, it's cold, but not nearly as bad as you're whining about, Bud."

"Shut it, newbie. I know your little bit of magic will keep you warm, but you need to save it for the real problem at hand. We've got a fight ahead, and I need you at full strength."

"Fine," the man grumbled, releasing the little trickle of magic he'd been using to protect himself from the elements. Suddenly, it was not nearly as comfortable as he'd been making it out to be.

Hozark and Demelza, on the other hand, showed no signs of discomfort despite their lack of magical heating. They'd both suffered through years of Ghalian training, and, while it was lightly snowing, this was in no way near the extremes they'd been forced to endure over the years. And for the man originally from this world, it was an almost laughably warm day.

"Don't worry, the city won't allow snow to be present," Hozark said. "The elder emmiks direct a modicum of power to ensure the strongest of the elements remain outside of the city boundaries."

"Then let's get going," Laskar said, impatiently.

"We shall momentarily. But first I must clear our tracks," Hozark replied, casting a basic blowing spell to cover their trail with a light dusting of the freshly fallen snow.

The weather would help them within the hour, covering any residual traces with its own white blanket. By then, they would be in the city, the former pirate and his partner waiting in a warm lodge while the Wampeh Ghalian did what they did best.

Infiltrate. Gather intel. Prepare themselves. And, of course, kill.

"About time! It's freezing out there. Barkeep, a draught of your finest!" the jovial man with ruddy red cheeks said as he stumbled into the watering hole nearest the barracks Visla Horvath's men resided in.

It was not a coincidence.

Demelza was out in her shimmer cloak, scouring the perimeter of the visla's grounds, noting guard numbers and positions as well as any other defensive issues they might have to deal with. Hozark, on the other hand, was putting his skills to work in a different way.

The Wampeh assassin looked nothing like himself, courtesy of a few carefully placed spells. In this climate, he didn't need to use as much magic to disguise his form. Bulky clothes did a lot of that for him. But his face and hands required some coloration and adjustment that simple makeup could not achieve.

The konus on his wrist gave off a trickle of magic, the device slowly feeding into his disguise. If he'd cast more of his own stolen power, it would have stayed in place easier. But up against not only a visla, but his former lover as well, he wanted to have every last drop of magic within him ready for whatever may come.

Hozark was liberal with his coin, as he was with his tongue, gradually bragging more and more about his successful trades in nearby systems to all who would listen to the drunkard. The deep-green Tslavar mercenaries, being inveterate thieves for the most part, paid particular attention to both the coin being so casually spent, as well as the tales being told.

In short order, the drunken trader had made fast friends with the group of dangerous men. But despite their rough looks and rougher attitudes, he didn't seem at all perturbed by them. In fact, as he drank more, he was downright fraternal with them.

The Tslavars were perfectly happy to accept the free drinks from the man with heavy pockets. Pockets that would soon be much lighter once they'd had their way with him. But for now, free drinks were the order of the day, and they all got happily buzzed, some so much so that they began to forget their nefarious plans and speak freely.

Alcohol was the great tongue loosener, no matter which world one was on, and this was no different. The Tslavars were a race of rather unsavory mercenaries, slave traders, and thugs, their services being utilized heavily by the Council of Twenty.

The steady stream of coin that brought them into the Council's services made them somewhat controllable allies, if not outright employees, though a great many were just that. And if the Council had their way, that number would only increase. And serving Visla Horvath here on Arkanis was just one of the many little ways the Council was slowly sinking its claws into the mercenary race and bringing them even further under their control.

Being rough and ready men, the Tslavars drank with gusto, constantly trying to one-up their new friend. A friend they did not realize was stone-sober, his alcohol materializing a hundred meters from their location with every drink he took. And as they bested one another in drink, so, too did they compete for the best story.

"It's usually boring," one of the visla's guards said.

"Boring? It sounds exciting," the inebriated guest said.

"Nah, not usually. But now it's finally heating up. There's going to be some *real* action at long last."

"Really? Like what?"

A sharp look from the highest-ranking of the men shut that line of conversation down rather quickly.

"I can't say, friend," the Tslavar replied. "But trust me, interesting things are afoot."

"Then I congratulate you on your improved fortunes! Another round!" Hozark called out.

Eventually, after many hours of tales of both glory and boredom, the drunken visitor rose to leave.

"Gentlemen, itssh been a pleassurrre," he slurred, hefting a heavy bag of coin onto the counter and settling his tab.

"Oh, but it's cold outside, friend," one of the men said. "You've been so generous, at least let me help you find your accommodations."

"Why, thank you. That's most kind," he replied, then staggered out into the night with his ill-intentioned guide.

Moments later, the five other men rose and left the establishment as well, following the darkened alleyways down which they knew their associate would be guiding their mark.

"Where are we going?" the hapless drunk asked as he was steered into a particularly poorly lit alleyway. "It's pretty dark this way."

"Nothing to worry about, friend. Just the magical illumination is weaker in this part of town. The wealthy save the power for the fancier areas. Nothing to be concerned about."

At that moment the other Tslavars emerged from the shadows. They'd hurried ahead and had been lying in wait. And now, their prize was in their grasp.

"You'll be wanting to hand over that coin now, *friend*," the Tslavar guide said.

The drunk looked around at the men on all sides. Some were quite large, and all were within arm's reach.

Perfect.

Even in the dim light, they could see the shine of his pointed canine teeth as he smiled. To their credit, they realized what he was quite quickly, having seen the visla's protector dispatch someone on more than one occasion. But it was already far too late for them.

And the alleyway provided plenty of places to hide their bodies.

Hozark made sure there was no trace of the violence he had imparted on the guards. In fact, in under a minute, the alleyway seemed almost cleaner than when he'd first stumbled upon it.

He had spent hours with the men, learning their names, their jobs, their accents, tics, and quirks. Everything he would need in order to blend in once he assumed their identity. Then the real work would begin.

Pulling a greater stream of stored magic from the konus band around his wrist, Hozark quietly spoke the words to the spells that carefully applied his magical disguise, slipping the Tslavar face and coloring into place so naturally that only a powerful visla could see through it. And even if that happened, by then he would be face-to-face with his target, and if that was the case, it would be too late for them anyway.

# CHAPTER SEVENTEEN

"Take these," Hozark said, tossing a pile of Tslavar uniforms to Uzabud and Laskar.

"Is that blood?" Laskar asked.

Uzabud smacked him on the back of the head. "What's wrong with you, man? Just wipe it off and get dressed."

Laskar's jovial nature faltered, a flash of something harder in his eyes.

"Shit. I'm sorry," Bud apologized. "But it was a stupid question."

"I was just asking. No need to get so testy," Laskar replied.

"Both of you, stop the yammering and get dressed. We will not have much time before these guards are missed. Demelza and I will enter via the main gates, but you lack the abilities we possess and would not fool the guards. Keep the hoods up against the weather, and stick to the shadows. When opportunity presents itself, try to make your way inside the compound, if you are able."

"What about her?" Laskar asked.

"Me?" the assassin asked, then muttered the arcane Wampeh spell that shifted her appearance to that of a Tslavar.

"Holy hell, that's spooky," he said.

"A skill of the Ghalian," the now Tslavar-green woman replied.

Given her relatively thick build, it was fairly easy to hide her curves by giving herself the illusion of a stocky man's shape. Once she'd done so, she was wearing a very convincing impression of a Tslavar guard.

Of course, she and Hozark were not actually wearing the captured uniforms. It would be impractical, and it would hinder their accessing all the myriad hidden pockets in their clothing that contained their many deadly wares. The only piece of actual Tslavar clothing they took were the overcloaks the guards wore against the chill.

Protection from the elements was one aspect of the reeking Tslavar material they would find useful. The other, they hoped would not come into play.

Hozark took his vespus blade and wrapped his shimmer cloak around it. "*Infarus occulo*," he said, the wrinkled material vanishing, hiding the shape of the sword with it.

He carefully strapped it to his back, adjusting the invisible weapon for easy access should he need to draw it in a hurry.

"Is that going to work?" Laskar asked.

"It is invisible, is it not?" he replied. "So long as no one bumps into me, the blade will not be revealed."

"Then you'd better not bump into anyone," his old friend suggested.

"Thank you, Bud. A wise suggestion," he replied with dry Wampeh sarcasm. "Demelza and I are heading in. If all goes well, we will see you soon. I have my skree on silent notice. Contact me only if it is absolutely necessary."

"Will do. And safe hunting," Bud said, garnering a brief nod from the Wampeh. Then the two assassins were gone.

. . .

"Who goes there?" the guard standing at the outermost gate to the visla's compound asked as the two shapes materialized out of the darkness.

"You know who it is, you wretched mendicant," Hozark said, matching the gruff tone and verbal style of the man whose identity he was currently using.

"Gozer? What are you doing out there? You were supposed to be on shift twenty minutes ago."

"We had something come up," the disguised Wampeh replied.

"You know Gunnar will be pissed."

"Trust me, it was a worthwhile delay," Hozark said, pulling a small pouch of coin from his pocket and tossing it to the man. "We spotted a fat traveler at the bar and lightened him of his load. That's your share. For watching the gate for us, of course."

He looked at the guard with a steady gaze. It only took the man a few seconds to assess the heft of the pouch and slip it into his own pocket.

"Well, in that case, I'm glad you were back on shift *on time*."

"As am I," Hozark replied with a convincing grin. "And if anyone asks, Yikza was back as well," he said, nodding toward Demelza.

"Of course," the guard said, patting his pocket.

"Have a safe shift," the assassin said as he stepped through the gate.

"Aren't they all?" the guard replied. "I'd almost wish for something to happen for a change. But with that pale bitch around, I don't think anyone's ever going to start trouble around here."

"Boredom is the price we pay," Hozark said with a laugh, then walked away.

"Well, that went well," Demelza said once they had passed through into the inner courtyard. "What's next?"

"Your guess is as good as mine," Hozark replied. "That was as far as our spies ever penetrated."

"So, we go in blind?"

"Basically. From here on, it's anyone's guess what lies ahead. But at least we won't suffer the same boredom as our new friend, eh?"

"That we will not," she replied, just as a rumbling shriek echoed off the stone walls. "In fact, I believe this will be far more interesting than we anticipated."

They both knew that sound, though they hadn't thought they'd hear it within the visla's walls. Zomoki. Two of them, by the sound of it. The beasts were large, with sharp teeth and claws, their mouths capable of spewing magical flames. The mere sight of a Zomoki was often enough to send chills down the spine of the most resolute fighter.

"Damn. I was not anticipating quite this degree of animal protection," Hozark quietly said. "But our ruse should work just the same."

"Let us hope you are correct," Demelza replied, pulling her cloak tight around her body.

The assassins walked casually toward the gate at the far end of the courtyard. It was their way into the inner chambers of the estate. All they had to do was pass the two beasts that stood on either side of the gate, sniffing the air.

There were golden control collars on each of their necks, of course. The magical bands would keep them from harming the visla's servants. One couldn't have one's guard pets devouring their staff, after all. But Hozark and Demelza were *not* the visla's staff. If the creatures decided to try to take a bite out of them, they would find the restraints utterly silent in reply.

This was the eventuality they had worn the cloaks for. Not this exact circumstance, of course. No one would have guessed there would be Zomoki guarding the gate. But some form of watch animal was fairly common. They just hoped the Tslavar stink on their outer garment would be enough to grant them passage.

The Zomoki were quite feral, Hozark noted as they drew closer. There was no gleam of intelligence in their eyes. Just raw animal instinct. The larger of the two, a blue-scaled beast with silver eyes, sniffed deep as they approached. It paused, then inhaled again. Something was churning in its primal brain, but before it could take an exploratory nibble at the pair, Hozark cast a minor shock spell, directing it at the creature's neck.

The jolt seemed to be enough to trick the animal into thinking its collar had activated. With a grumble, it settled back on its haunches and let the two disguised Wampeh pass.

They had just entered the inner portion of Visla Horvath's estate when Hozark felt something familiar. And unexpected. A bit of the stolen magic he still had flowing within him.

"There are some of Emmik Rostall's possessions here," he said. "I feel his power stored in them."

"Should they be here? Didn't you just kill the man?"

"I did. And it was Visla Tumertz who was believed poised to take up his slack. But this feels odd. Older. As if the emmik had sent these charged devices here *before* he was slain. And if that is the case, he and Visla Horvath had a much different relationship than any had known."

"That is rather interesting," Demelza said.

"Indeed. And somewhat disturbing. If they were working together prior to that contract, it would seem possible that Horvath was working in concert with Rostall to upend the Council and seize more power for themselves."

"That would be bad."

"Yes. Far worse than we realized," Hozark said.

"There was some talk," Demelza offered. "Rumors I became aware of. It was while in the service of Orkut that I heard this, mind you. But he has some very powerful clients."

"Understandable. What did you hear?"

"Nothing concrete. But in one of his discussions about the Council and their constant expansion plans, he said he wasn't sure, but it seemed there was another visla pulling strings at a far higher level than any realized. An enormously powerful caster who was using the others to further his own interests, but without their even realizing it."

Hozark's interest was piqued, to say the least. "He did not mention this to me."

"Nor would he. It was a theory. Nothing proven yet. But I do know he had committed resources to finding out if the rumors held any truth."

"Do we know who this alleged visla mastermind is?" the master assassin asked.

"A visla who has managed to stay largely out of the public eye. A person by the name Maktan."

"Never heard of him."

"Or *her*. The visla's gender was not certain," she corrected.

Hozark's brow furrowed slightly. This was a wrinkle he would have to deal with, he feared. But now was not the time.

"We will discuss this further when the task at hand is complete," he said. "For now, we must complete this mission. Come."

The two then padded off in search of their target, one of them anxious about confronting a visla, the other preoccupied about the woman protecting him.

# CHAPTER EIGHTEEN

The pair of assassins made good time inside the visla's estate, their Tslavar disguises providing them a fair amount of defense against unwanted scrutiny. But there was a problem.

"You see it, do you not?" Hozark asked.

"I do. The uniforms are different this far into the property."

"Yes. We shall require new identities if we mean to progress."

"I spotted a suitable staff area in which to stash any bodies we may need to dispose of. But maybe we should use our shimmer cloaks instead."

"Not yet. A powerful and alert visla would almost certainly sense and see through them anyway. Our disguise spells use far less magic and will be less likely to raise his attention until it is too late."

"Very well," Demelza relented. "But we really should—"

A vibration shook Hozark's hip. He held up his hand, then took his skree and switched it to audible.

"Red Scout to Red Leader, we are inside," Bud's voice said quietly.

"Already?" Hozark replied, surprised. "And what is this 'Red Scout' you speak of?"

"Just code names. Code names are cool."

"Bud. You digress."

"Yeah, sorry. Anyway, we found another way in over toward the back of the compound."

"Really? Hmm, that is odd. One would think it would have been better guarded," the assassin noted.

"It was, but there was a delay when there was a shift change. Looks like someone was running late, and it gave us a window of opportunity. We barely made it, but we're inside now. Have you made contact yet?"

"No, we are still working our way toward our target," the assassin replied.

"Okay. You keep doing your thing. We'll come find you."

The skree went silent just as many loud voices could be heard ringing out from a nearby room.

"We must hurry. A major shift change seems about to occur. It is only a matter of time before the missing guards are noted," Hozark said, drawing an enchanted blade from a hidden pocket as he headed toward the door.

"The time for stealth seems to be at an end," Demelza said with a grin. "I will cast my most robust silencing spells on the threshold. That should buy us a little time, at least."

Hozark waited until she spoke the words, the angry voices falling silent as the spell took hold of the doorway before he passed through. She uttered them in a quiet voice, but, like all spells, the words were the key. If they were not intoned, the spell would fail. All but a handful of the most powerful faced this constraint. And more than just the words, the *intent* behind them had to align perfectly.

Fortunately, Demelza was a skilled caster. It was a good thing, as the dozen Tslavar mercenaries were about to make a lot of noise. And those would be the last sounds to ever leave their mouths.

Hozark was still in disguise when he burst into the room.

The startled men reached for weapons, a few drawing magic from their konuses, before they realized it was one of their own and relaxed.

That was their first mistake.

The second was allowing the man who wore the right uniform but who seemed just a little bit off to draw near to them unchallenged.

"Hey, what's with the--" a burly Tslavar began to say.

His query was cut short by Hozark's flashing blade nearly taking his head clean off.

"Assassin!"

The other men leapt into action. They were actually a rather skilled group. Far more experienced than the guards Hozark had disposed of in town. And, it seemed, there was another adjacent room in which their comrades had been resting. The numbers were suddenly very much not in the assassin's favor.

A wave of armed guards rushed into the fray, the Wampeh cutting them down as fast as he was able. The noise of battle was immense. He sincerely hoped Demelza's spell was strong enough for this unexpected increase in volume.

He always worked alone. Even when he and Samara had been an item. But on this occasion, his hand had been forced by the wily swordsmith. And about his unwanted sidekick, despite the lingering sting of having lost Enok so recently, when he caught sight of Demelza whirling into the fray like an armed dervish, he suddenly felt a little flash of gladness that Orkut had demanded she join him.

She was good. *Really* good.

She may have possessed a stocky physique, but Demelza was a Wampeh Ghalian, and she effortlessly flowed and killed with the skill one would expect of a woman half her size. The Tslavars were hopelessly outmatched by the deadly duo, and in less than a minute the pair had sent nearly two dozen highly trained guards to their final slumber.

"There is no way this many will not be missed," Hozark noted, wiping his blade on a fallen man's tunic as he surveyed the carnage.

Demelza had come to a similar conclusion. "We will have to accelerate our advance. And greatly, at that."

"Agreed. It appears we must split up to cover more ground, and with great haste," he added.

"I will cast a blockading spell on the main door once I exit. It won't buy us much time, but it should delay their discovery and help buy us a little time," Demelza said.

"And I will do the same on the other door, though I am saving as much of my strength as possible for Visla Horvath and Samara."

Demelza cocked her head, reaching out to the air around them, scanning with her magic. "Have you sensed her yet? I can feel traces of Horvath's power, so he must be somewhere nearby, but we Ghalian are much harder to detect."

"No, nothing from her. Not yet, anyway."

"Perhaps we have gotten lucky and she is off world on an errand for the visla," Demelza mused.

"Or she is merely lurking. Hiding her power. She always was an exceptional lurker," Hozark said, a hint of remorse to his voice. "Regardless, we must part ways here. Call if you find either of them, and I shall do the same."

"I will. And good hunting," she said, turning toward the empty hallway.

"And to you," he said, then took off in the opposite direction.

# CHAPTER NINETEEN

Surprisingly, the hallways were empty as Hozark followed their twisting maze deeper into the complex. Most would be hopelessly lost by this point, but the master assassin had already committed every turn to memory, down to the number of steps taken between intersections.

He was a Ghalian. He was one of the Five. For him, this was second nature. As simple as breathing.

The visla's power was a tricky thing, the sense of it flickering in and out as he moved through the estate. Somehow, it was irregular in its strength, making it extremely hard to pinpoint its origin. But after a great deal of focusing, Hozark finally homed in on a thread of magic that seemed stronger than the rest. More consistent.

"There you are," he quietly said, a little smile reaching the corners of his mouth.

One way or another, this was coming to a head. And soon. Right through the next doorway, it seemed.

Hozark drew a tiny bit more magic from his konus and affixed the disguise as well as he ever had. He just needed to get close enough to land a disabling blow before his ruse was noted, then he could finish the visla at his leisure. Senses on high alert, he eased through the threshold, acting as normal as any guard would be on their regular duty.

There the man was, no more than twenty meters from him, sitting quietly on a large chair at the far end of the room. And from what he could see, he was alone. Hozark was just formulating the next phase of his plan when the door behind him slammed shut and sealed with a magical ward.

That did not make his heart rate rise, nor did it make his adrenaline surge. But the velvety voice he heard a moment later did.

"Hello, Hozark," a lithe Wampeh said, materializing from the long shadows near the wall.

"Hello, Samara. It has been quite a while."

"Yes, it has."

"Still lurking, I see."

"Old habits die hard."

"As does the woman who possesses them, it seems," he replied, the faintest glimmer of memory in his eyes.

Samara didn't react. In fact, she was as cold as ice standing there between her former lover and her employer. She was entirely unflustered, and yet, for just a split second, he could have sworn he saw a flicker of something on her end too.

"I heard the order was sending someone," the seated man said, while his guardian slowly paced before him.

Hozark was on full defense, every cell in his body ready to fight. Samara was a deadly foe, but now that he was close enough to properly sense him, he knew her employer was far more dangerous than she was. Magically-speaking, that is.

"So, you're the infamous Hozark, eh?" the visla mused.

Hozark's lips remained sealed as he assessed his options. They were far fewer than he would have liked.

"You may as well lose the disguise. I'm sure you'll want that little bit of power at your disposal," the visla said. "You know, I've heard much about you."

The assassin didn't even glance at Samara. "I'm sure you have."

"The same man who ended Emmik Rostall, I assume?"

This *was* surprising. That was the freshest of events, and the odds of word traveling so far so fast were slim to none. The visla enjoyed watching the barely noticeable hints of confusion play out on his would-be attacker's face.

"Oh, you are surprised I know this?"

"Not at all," Hozark bluffed. "I know you and Emmik Rostall were working together to wrest more power from the Council of Twenty. A ballsy move, that. Trying to take from the hand that feeds you."

The visla laughed. "Oh, he *is* a spirited one. You were correct, Samara. And you are right. Rostall and I did have dealings with one another. Projects in the works that you have most inconveniently brought to a premature end. But that isn't all that ended prematurely, is it? A certain aspirant, if I'm not mistaken? Enok, wasn't it? And the Balamar waters? Amazing I'd not heard of Rostall's possessing any, that sneaky fellow," he said, a look of malicious joy in his eyes. "Quite a terrible way to go for your kind, I'd imagine. The whole combusting thing must have been quite painful."

Hozark's jaw twitched, but he kept the rest of his expression placid as his mind raced.

"You wonder how I know all of this, I'm sure. Well, my dangerous friend, in addition to my own agents, my lovely associate here still has her fingers in the Ghalian spy network. Of course, that is privileged information only the two of us are privy to. But I only share this juicy tidbit as you will not be leaving here alive to tell anyone."

"It is you who won't be drawing breath when this is done,"

Hozark said, hoping to draw the man into a direct conflict where he might at least *hope* to land a lucky blow before being struck down by his power. He just had to goad him into doing something foolish. "When I've finished with you," Hozark continued, "all of your fortune and power, all that you have built will—"

"Blah, blah, blah. Samara, please dispose of this pest."

The tall woman slowly drew the faintly glowing blue sword from the sheath on her back. With a little burst of magical intent, she focused her power and sent it into the blade, causing it to spark brighter, pulsing with energy.

"You've fed recently, I see," Hozark said, pushing aside the shimmer cloak hiding his own weapon and pulling his own vespus blade free.

The new sword was bright even in full light, crackling with fresh magic. At that, Samara actually looked surprised. She'd possessed one of the only known vespus blades for so long, encountering another was more than just a novelty. It was a near impossibility.

She squinted as she reached out to sense the sword's power. Her eyes widened slightly. "Is that an Orkut blade?"

Hozark nodded.

"I thought he was dead."

"Obviously not," he replied.

"The craftsmanship is exquisite, I must admit. But it is of little consequence. Swordplay was never your strong suit," she teased.

"Oh, but I've been practicing," was all he said before launching through the air in a furious attack.

The magical blades clashed, bright sparks and bolts of displaced magic showering the room.

Hozark had indeed been practicing. A lot, in the many years since he believed Samara had fallen. And that hard work was showing, for while she had maintained her prior, impressive skills, he had leveled up. Repeatedly.

It had been a long time since the visla's right hand had actually been challenged like this, and the power user was greatly enjoying the contest. In fact, Visla Horvath was beaming like a fool, thoroughly enjoying the novel gladiatorial spectacle. This one was actually giving his favorite killer a run for her money. Of course, if it looked like his precious Wampeh might fall, he would step in, naturally.

Samara fought with a relaxed posture, even though it might cost her a bit more energy as she used her power to deflect his attacks, for she knew her master's mind. She was in no real danger. She had a visla watching her back. The outcome was already decided.

The two covered most of the chamber as they fought, the quick attacks of the Wampeh Ghalian and the deadly force channeled through their equally deadly vespus blades evenly matched. They knew each other's styles intimately after a lifetime of training together. Every movement was matched by its counter, and the pair continuously arrived at a stalemate.

Most such fights would have been over in seconds. On the rarest of occasions, a Ghalian master might require up to a minute. This fight, however, dragged on and on as both assassins dug deep into their power, draining what they'd stored in their swords as well as themselves.

"Stop fighting, Hozark," Samara said as their blades locked once again.

"Now, why would I do that?" he replied through clenched teeth.

"I can make it quick and painless. You needn't suffer," she replied, a tiny flash of sympathy in her eye. "You've fought well. Better than that. But now it's time to just give up. You know the outcome here is already decided, no matter how well you fight."

A little smile flashed across Hozark's lips. "Oh, is it?"

It wasn't his words so much as the smile that made Samara

falter. She knew him too well. Something was in play. Something was up.

She quickly unlocked her blade from his and pushed back, creating space to regroup. With an opponent like him, she couldn't be sloppy even for an instant. It was then that she turned and saw what he'd been distracting her from.

The visla sat askew in his mighty chair, his head tilted to the side as Demelza drained him of his blood and power, her shimmer cloak fallen aside in the process.

The visla had been so gleefully distracted by the violent display his favorite killer was putting on that he failed to sense the cloaked assassin behind him until it was too late.

Samara spun back to Hozark, shock and rage in her eyes. "You never work with another! Never! Not even with me!"

"Times change, Sam," he replied with a wistful smile. "Now, about that giving up proposition of yours."

She knew she was screwed. Utterly, completely screwed. So she did the one thing she could.

"Not a chance," she said, then unloaded a massive magical attack, triggering a cascade of hidden magical traps in the room that forced Hozark and his bitch partner to divert their attention and focus all of their magic on protecting themselves, leaving her a window to escape.

"That was a cheap trick," Demelza said when the barrage subsided, licking her bloody lips. "I'll have to remember it."

The visla twitched slightly in her grip. Apparently, he wasn't quite finished yet. Surprised at his resilience, she then leaned in once more to finish the job once and for all while Hozark took off running after his prey.

# CHAPTER TWENTY

Hozark moved as if he were a man possessed, and in some ways, he was. It had been nearly ten years since Samara had died, yet seeing her now, even after so long, her presence felt as natural as breathing.

And it was her breathing he was about to end.

Thoughts and emotions he believed long buried were surfacing once more. Inky specters of a hurt that physical salves could not heal. When Samara had died those many years ago, Hozark had shed the only tears to escape his eyes since childhood. In private, of course, and only during the briefest lapse in his Ghalian will. But it had happened. Her death had hit him hard.

And he was about to kill her again.

But, maybe, just maybe, there was the chance he could capture her. Take her back to the order. Somehow bring her back into the fold. But first, he would have to catch her.

A flash of her alabaster skin rounding the corner at the far end of the passage was all he could see of his quarry. But he was a man on a mission, and it was all he needed. Hozark increased his pace, pushing himself even harder to overtake her.

He rounded the corner, which he recalled from his incursion led into a small outdoor courtyard. The hair on his neck tingled, and even though he was at a full run, he threw his body aside in a diving tumble, rolling to his feet several yards away.

The assassin looked up at the faintly glowing blade embedded in the wall where his head would have been. Samara yanked it free with a grunt and charged him. Not yelling like a banshee, but with silent intensity, as was the Ghalian way. Even in the throes of battle, it was hard to get a peep out of the stealthy killers.

A trio of Tslavar guards who had stumbled upon the scene raced into the fray, casting deadly spells with their konuses despite the closeness of the quarters. Normally, only conventional weapons would be used in such confines. The risk of a spell going awry and slaying one of your comrades was simply too great.

The danger was even greater if the battle was taking place aboard a ship out in space. One wrong spell and both sides of the conflict could be hurtled into the void. More than one battle had abruptly ended due to a carelessly cast spell.

The Wampeh's sword still possessed a fair charge of magic, which he drew upon instinctively, using its power to counter the weaker konus-driven spells as he hacked the casters down with brutal efficiency.

The men had rushed headfirst into far more than a mere fight between two Wampeh, and their interference was remedied far quicker than they'd have imagined possible. But a motivated Ghalian is a dangerous thing, and this one was *very* motivated.

Samara hadn't waited even a beat as the Tslavars fell, pressing her attack with near reckless abandon. Hozark parried her flashing strokes, deflecting her vespus blade with his own.

It was a powerful, elegant weapon she possessed, slimmer than his, designed for a feminine hand. It had been handed down to her when a favored mentor fell in combat, and it knew few equals.

But his blade was newer. Newer and stronger. Orkut's skill was unrivaled in that regard, and the time and effort seeking the man out had proven well worth the expenditure. It wasn't a great advantage the magical weapon gave him, but as they fought, it became clear that minuscule edge would be enough, and they both knew it.

They knew it, but Samara was not one to give up. Not now. Not ever.

It would take time to wear her down enough to even think about attempting to capture rather than kill her, but Hozark was willing to put in the effort no matter how tired his sword-wielding arms were becoming.

"There are too many of them!" a voice called out. It was Uzabud, his voice slightly muffled as Hozark's skree was still in his pocket. "They've got us pinned down. It was a trap!"

Hozark broke from his engagement, taking several steps back, but remaining ever-vigilant as he pulled the skree from his pocket. "Where are you, Bud?" he asked over the device.

"The kitchens. Me and Laskar took a few down, but we're totally screwed here! Hurry!"

Hozark's gaze remained locked with Samara's. He saw the flicker of a smile in her eyes as he mulled the dilemma.

"Hold fast. I'm coming to you," he finally replied, the smile in Samara's eyes spreading to her lips. With a wink, she turned and ran. Reluctantly, he did the same, charging back into the building's depths to save his friend.

The grounds were buzzing with activity. Apparently, the visla's body had been discovered, sending the place into a chaotic response. The visla was dead. What were they supposed to do? With their patron gone, who was in charge?

For Tslavars, the easiest choice was their natural instinct. Fight.

Hozark didn't have the magic to waste reapplying his disguise. His battle with Samara had taken far more out of him than he'd have liked. So, it was old-fashioned bladed carnage he meted out to those foolish enough to cross his path.

He moved quickly toward the kitchens, leaving a trail of death and dismemberment in his wake. Bud's voice could be heard casting spells in a frantic attempt at defense. Laskar was trying to help as well, but even with a konus aiding him, his magic was terribly inefficient.

The assassin moved to attempt to flank the main body of guards pressing his two comrades when a blast of magic rocked the chamber.

Demelza, full of stolen power—a *visla*'s power, no less—strode into the room and unleashed the magic she'd taken from Horvath only minutes before. He had been a powerful man, and it was their former employer's magic that was now slaying his guards as they tried to flee.

Hozark was pleased to see just how talented the woman truly was. A great ally, indeed, it would appear.

Fortune smiled upon a few of the guards, who somehow found cover as the magic flew. Those then ran like the wind and managed to escape. But the main body of the group was left shattered by the assassin's killing spells.

"They'll be back with reinforcements," Uzabud said, rising from his sheltered spot.

"I know," Hozark replied. "And we need to get airborne immediately. Samara will undoubtedly make a run for it, given her patron is dead. But we can still intercept."

"We need to go while the going's good, then," Bud replied. "Come on! Laskar, you okay? We gotta move!"

"Yeah, I'll live," the copilot said, brushing debris from his clothes.

"Demelza, take the lead and clear a path. I will cover our rear. We go straight for the ship, no detours."

"As you wish, Hozark," she said, then took off at a run, the others close on her heels.

They made good time to the ship, and judging by the pristine layer of snow that had fallen around it, none had disturbed their shimmer-cloaked craft. The four piled into the vessel with haste and prepared for flight, Hozark's Drookonus firmly in place, powering the craft.

"That was some show back there," Laskar said as Bud guided the ship into the sky. "All that magic, I guess that means you got him?"

Demelza merely nodded as she continued wiping the blood of battle from her hands with a rag she carried for just such occasions.

"Wow," the copilot continued. "I'd heard about how you guys take someone's power, but I've never actually seen a Wampeh do that in person. What's it like? And, he's—I mean, he *was* a pretty powerful visla. Why couldn't he stop you?"

"Because he was distracted by Hozark and Samara's combat," Demelza replied. "He was so focused on the fight unfolding before him that he did not sense me approach under cover of my shimmer cloak."

"A shimmer cloak did him in? Wild. Absolutely wild," Laskar said.

"Is that her?" Bud asked, pointing toward a distant streak lifting off from the other side of the city. "Looks like that ship's in quite a hurry."

Hozark recognized the style immediately. It was an older model, but it was a Wampeh Ghalian shimmer ship. Only, it was apparently not at full power as it remained visible. Most shimmers did in space, anyway. Only the most powerful of them could effectively cloak themselves there. And she had used a *lot* of power in their fight.

Uzabud pushed the ship hard, pulling a great deal of the stored magic from the Drookonus. Hozark had spared no expense on the device, and it was precisely at moments like this that the foresight paid off. The pursuing craft rapidly gained on the fleeing ship as it shot straight up into the darkness of space.

It seemed Samara didn't have enough power for even a minor jump, but was instead attempting a speed run, hoping to get herself far enough away to avoid notice. In that, however, she had failed.

"I've got a shot," Laskar said from his seat. The craft was small, but no Ghalian would travel without a robustly powered weapons station full of deadly magic. "Should I cast?"

Hozark stared at the ship they were rapidly closing on in silence.

"Hozark?" Bud said, but the Wampeh remained silent. "Fuck it. Open fire," he commanded. "Stop that ship."

"Casting," Laskar announced, then let loose a burst of magical turbulence, drawing a substantial amount of the stored power from their craft. Far more than intended, in fact.

The spell was much more potent than the poor man had meant to cast, and it flew true. Had she been performing evasive maneuvers, perhaps Samara would have avoided the spell, but in an all-out speed run, she had put herself in jeopardy, and that risk was now proving a poor, fatal choice.

The spell slammed into her ship with exponentially more force than Laskar had intended, the craft exploding into millions of tiny bits from the power.

"Whoa," the gunner gasped.

"Nice shooting, Laskar," Bud said. "A bit excessive, maybe, but nice."

"It was a job well done," Demelza added. "Both the visla and the rogue Ghalian have been eliminated. The order will be pleased."

"Yes, they will," Hozark replied through teeth he didn't realize he'd been clenching as he watched the wreckage spread out and drift off into space.

. . .

"Demelza, it has been quite a while," Corann said upon seeing not one but two Wampeh Ghalian enter the training house. "You were assisting Orkut last I heard, were you not?"

"Yes. But I was tasked with helping Hozark fulfill his contract."

"I see," the woman replied, turning to Hozark. Her eyes fell upon the scabbard on his back. "So, he *did* make you one, I see."

"He did," Hozark replied, unsheathing the sword and handing it to her.

"Magnificent," Corann said as she caressed the blade as a non-assassin might touch a lover.

She focused, pushing a tiny fraction of her magic into the weapon. It crackled to life, glowing happily from even the tiny influx of power.

"A most impressive vespus blade, indeed. Master Orkut outdid himself."

"I would have to agree," Hozark replied.

"We got her, Corann. Not only the visla, but Samara as well," Demelza informed the leader of the Five.

"Is this true? You saw her fall?"

"Yes," Hozark said. "Her craft was utterly destroyed."

"Then that chapter is finally over," Corann said. "Again. Thank you for your assistance, Demelza. You performed admirably."

"I was glad to be of use."

She turned to Hozark. "As for you, there will be many contracts in coming months. But why don't you take a brief respite. I think after this particular endeavor, it might do you some good."

"I may just do that," he replied, then took his leave, heading for an empty room with a warm bath and a cool bed.

Samara was dead. He'd watched her ship break apart with

his own eyes. But despite what they'd all seen, he was nevertheless uncertain. She'd died once before, after all, and he couldn't help but entertain that lingering doubt.

A short while later, cleaned of the blood of battle, he lay his weary body down between the welcoming sheets of his bed and felt the strain of the past weeks slowly ebb away.

Moments later the exhaustion finally took hold and he began to drift off to sleep, where, if he was lucky, he would perhaps see Samara one last time.

# PREVIEW: THE VESPUS BLADE

## SPACE ASSASSINS 2

Normally, the light of the nearly full moon would have reflected brightly from the Ootaki woman's golden hair. The natural magic storing property of her kind's resplendent locks made them something to behold under the right circumstances.

These, however, were not the right circumstances. Mud and debris werematted into her hair and were likewise smeared over most of her body. Her hasty escape had been the cause of that. It was also the reason she was still free.

For the time being at least.

The woman ran on even faster than before, pushing herself far beyond her own perceived limitations. Ootaki might have been capable of storing massive quantities of magic in their hair, but as a people, they were unable to tap into it themselves. A cruel joke of fate, for the mostly enslaved race.

But not all Ootaki were slaves. Some small pockets of free folk still existed at the periphery of the systems. Places where the peaceful, pale-yellow-skinned people with their golden hair could live unmolested by ruffians and scoundrels.

Usually, at least.

Hers had been a tranquil existence. A quiet life with her

friends and family, all living in a small commune in a quiet corner of a quiet world.

Then the horror fell upon them, shattering all semblance of peace they had ever known. And it wasn't just a random group of pirates or thieves. Those they could hide from as they'd done in the past. But not this time. This time, they'd been discovered by Tslavars.

They were a disgusting race of mercenaries. Slave traders. Strong arms for hire, working for the highest bidder. The deep-green-skinned men and women were more than that, however.

They took great pleasure in their profession, making them even worse than mere thugs for hire. They *enjoyed* the dirty work. And that made them a particularly popular tool of the Council of Twenty as that group of power users strove to expand their control over the known systems.

And that was what they were doing here, undoubtedly. Rounding up the magical beings for their masters. All of them to be collared and enslaved, their hair to be charged with even more magic until such time as it was ready to be harvested, even though some of that power would be lost in the shearing process.

The first cut was always the most potent, and for that reason, the younger Ootaki were a great prize. One that could be groomed their whole life until a rainy day. Or a day their owner *wanted* it to rain. Fire and brimstone, that is, for their harvested magic could be a fearsome thing.

But to preserve the power without loss upon cutting, an Ootaki could give their hair freely. It was rarely done, though, and their locks always knew their owner's intent, even if they did say the words, "Freely given."

If their heart wasn't truly in it, the hair would know and only be a tiny fraction stronger than that taken by force.

There were tales that Ootaki hair given not only freely, but out of love, held immense power, exponentially greater than what it appeared to initially contain, binding it forever to the recipient. But that was no more than a myth. A legend. For Ootaki could not use their own kind's power, and giving it in love to another of their race, even out of love, would have no effect.

A ship roared through the air nearby, powered by a team of Drooks, the enslaved men and women focusing their particular flavor of magic to make the craft fly. Free Drooks were even more rare than free Ootaki, for without them, interstellar travel would be impossible.

Such was the way of this magical galaxy.

The golden-haired woman raced through the sparse woods that bordered the fields at the far end of her people's enclave. Her clothing was torn, her pale-yellow skin bleeding from the myriad scrapes and abrasions acquired in her hasty flight. And, of course, her hair was a mess of dirt and grime.

A faint whiff of fresh moisture greeted her nose and exhausted lungs. The river. It was close by.

She pushed on, racing as fast as her feet could carry her on the uneven ground, even as the trees grew thicker close to the water's edge. Her father had told her to run. To run far and find water. Only there could she hide her scent from any tracking animals the invaders might possess.

Another ship approached, much lower and much closer this time. The young woman quickly jumped into the muddy water at the river's shore and tucked herself beneath a partially submerged log near the water's edge. It was not a moment too soon, for footsteps could be heard growing near. *Many* of them. And not all of them belonging to the men and women hunting her.

There was something else. A sound besides that of the clomping boots of the mercenaries. When she heard the nearby snuffling of the Tslavars' beasts, she realized her father had been correct in his assumption. Trackers, no doubt.

She shifted ever so slowly, allowing herself the tiniest of glimpses of the animals padding along the shoreline. They weren't terribly large, nor were they particularly fierce in appearance. Nothing like their massive, distant cousins often used as guards for royal families of particular note and wealth.

But these smaller versions, with their wiry hair and long snouts, had a keen sense of smell, and for that they served the Tslavars well. And there was more to them than mere animal tracking.

*These* animals, in addition to sweat and fear, could also sense magic. And that was something the Ootaki girl had in abundance. Fortunately for her, the flowing waters of this world possessed ambient magic of their own, though minor. Nevertheless, it muddied her scent, preventing them from getting a proper fix on her.

She felt a tug on her head. Her hair was of great length, having never been cut, as was the Ootaki way, and the weight of it in the water was threatening to pull her farther out into the fast-moving current. The same current that was also beginning to rinse away some of the mud caked in her hair.

She felt her grip on the slippery log failing as the pull of the river drew her farther into its depths. Any moment now, she would be swept free, a golden-haired treasure for all to see. She clung as tightly as she could, but as she had feared, the river finally took her into its embrace.

Only not as she'd imagined.

Rather than floating along the surface, making an easy target for the hunters along the shoreline, she was hit by a piece of debris and pulled underwater, swept out to the middle of the torrent.

Drowning was suddenly a very real possibility, and as her lungs burned with the need for air, the thought of slavery was beginning to sound a lot better than that alternative.

Pulling frantically, she felt her head begin to go light as stars coalesced at the periphery of her vision. Her body was starting to go weak, the lack of oxygen taking its toll. She was going to drown, she realized.

Fear shot through her body, the surge of adrenaline giving her the energy for one last burst of strength. With a final, mighty pull, she freed her hair from whatever it was she'd been caught up by and burst through the surface, gulping in huge lungfuls of air.

She expected to hear shouts, then be snatched from the water. Instead, she heard nothing. Drained, she collapsed at the shoreline.

"Where am I?" she wondered as she pulled herself from the waters.

It seemed that the current in the middle of the river was far faster than that at the shoreline, and she had been transported a great distance in a short time. Far enough that her home was now a significant distance away, in fact.

Scared, wet, and alone, she sloshed from the shore into the relative cover of the woods nearby. Her hair was golden once more, she realized. She had to get out of the moonlight before the shine caught someone's eye.

Deeper into the woods she walked, fighting back tears with every step. She was worse than lost. She was alone. *Truly* alone, for her entire family had been captured just after her father told her to flee. She'd never seen such urgency in his eyes before, and she had reacted immediately without question. It was the only reason she'd escaped.

And now she was on her own. On her own and far from home, walking through woods she'd never before set foot in.

She moved farther from the rushing water and stopped to listen. Far away, the faint sound of Tslavar voices could be heard carrying over the water. But sound was funny like that, and those men could be miles away.

It was quiet here. Quieter than back home. There were no

laughs of children, nor the sounds of livestock and those tending them. Just her own faint footsteps on the soft soil.

This would not be easy, but she owed it to her father to survive. To make sure at least someone could recount what had happened here this night. With her will renewed and her back straightened, she began walking, her home to her back. She could never return. That was simply how it would be. But she would make the most of it.

A magical stun spell slammed her to the ground, nearly knocking her unconscious.

Snarling Tslavar mercenaries stepped out of the shadows, shedding their magical camouflage. They wore shimmer cloaks, though not very good ones. Adding to that was their lack of proficiency in the spells to utilize them, which led to mediocre camouflage at best.

But for the distracted Ootaki girl, they had proven more than enough and served their purpose well in the dim light. Certainly, any with a fair degree of training would have spotted them, but a scared Ootaki girl with no off-world experience didn't stand a chance.

"Skree back to Captain Moratz we've got another one," a Tslavar said as he loomed over the fallen girl.

"She's young. And her hair is long. We'll get a nice bonus for this one," his associate said.

"Yeah, and it's about time," his friend replied. "Work's been picking up lately, and I gotta say, I'm getting a bit antsy for some shore leave."

"I couldn't agree more. I'm looking forward to a stiff drink and a warm woman, once we get paid."

"You said it," the other Tslavar said as he threw the young woman over his shoulder. "Come on, let's get this one back. We might get lucky and find a few more if we hurry."

The two carried her back to the hastily constructed pen the other captured Ootaki had been corralled into and unfastened the gate. A golden control collar was slapped around her neck, magically sealing into an unbroken band, keeping her under the control of her owner. She was no longer free. She was now someone's property.

Just like all of the other slaves in the galaxy.

# ALSO BY SCOTT BARON

**Standalone Novels**

Living the Good Death

**The Clockwork Chimera Series**

Daisy's Run

Pushing Daisy

Daisy's Gambit

Chasing Daisy

Daisy's War

**The Dragon Mage Series**

Bad Luck Charlie

Space Pirate Charlie

Dragon King Charlie

Magic Man Charlie

Star Fighter Charlie

Portal Thief Charlie

Rebel Mage Charlie

Warp Speed Charlie

Checkmate Charlie

**The Space Assassins Series**

The Interstellar Slayer

The Vespus Blade

The Ghalian Code

Death From the Shadows

Hozark's Revenge

**The Warp Riders Series**

Deep Space Boogie

Belly of the Beast

**Odd and Unusual Short Stories:**

The Best Laid Plans of Mice: An Anthology

Snow White's Walk of Shame

The Tin Foil Hat Club

Lawyers vs. Demons

The Queen of the Nutters

Lost & Found

# ABOUT THE AUTHOR

A native Californian, Scott Baron was born in Hollywood, which he claims may be the reason for his rather off-kilter sense of humor.

Before taking up residence in Venice Beach, Scott first spent a few years abroad in Florence, Italy before returning home to Los Angeles and settling into the film and television industry, where he has worked as an on-set medic for many years.

Aside from mending boo-boos and owies, and penning books and screenplays, Scott is also involved in indie film and theater scene both in the U.S. and abroad.

CPSIA information can be obtained
at www.ICGtesting.com
Printed in the USA
BVHW061517221222
654839BV00003B/44